THE WAR GOD'S WORLD

Barrakesh is the gateway between north and south on Mars. Long ago, when Valkis and Jekkara were seats of empire and not thieves' dens, Barrakesh had been the meeting place for the rich caravans traveling all of Mars. It is a city of countless years and countless strangers.

Now Mars is a dying planet, dried up and hostile, but Barrakesh is still the meeting place—for the Keshi hillmen; the nomads of Shun; tomb-robbers from the south; men and not-quite men from the Low Canals' deserted and silent towns; cosmopolitan sophisticates from Kahora and the Trade Cities.

Everyone is free to come and go in Barrakesh—everyone but the Terrans, for even a dying planet will kill to protect its secrets and what treasure it has left.

D1739219

THE COMING OF THE TERRANS

by

LEIGH BRACKETT

ACE BOOKS, INC.
1120 Avenue of the Americas
New York, N.Y. 10036

Leigh Brackett has also written:

THE SECRET OF SINHARAT *and*
PEOPLE OF THE TALISMAN (M-101)

THE SWORD OF RHIANNON (F-422)

FOREWORD

To some of us, Mars has always been the Ultima Thule, the golden Hesperides, the ever-beckoning land of compelling fascination. Voyagers, electronic and human, have begun the business of reducing these dreams to cold, hard, ruinous fact. But as we know, in the affairs of men and Martians, mere fact runs a poor second to Truth, which is mighty and shall prevail. Therefore I offer you these legends of Old Mars as true tales, inviting all dreary realities to keep a respectful distance.

I can vouch for every one of these adventures. After all, I was there.

CHRONOLOGY

1998: THE BEAST-JEWEL OF MARS

I

BURK WINTERS remained in the passenger section while the *Starflight* made her landing at Kahora Port. He did not think that he could bear to see another man, not even one he liked as much as he did Johnny Niles, handle the controls of the ship that had been his for so long.

He did not wish even to say goodbye to Johnny, but there was no avoiding it. The young officer was waiting for him as he came down the ramp, and the deep concern he felt was not hidden in the least by his casually hearty grin.

Johnny held out his hand. "So long, Burk. You've earned this leave. Have fun with it."

Burk Winters looked out over the vast tarmac that spread for miles across the ochre desert. An orderly, roaring confusion of trucks and flatcars and men and ships—ore ships, freighters, tramps, sleek liners like the *Starflight*, bearing the colors of three planets and a dozen colonies, but still arrogantly and predominantly Terran.

Johnny followed his gaze and said softly, "It always gives you a thrill, doesn't it?"

Winters did not answer. Miles away, safe from the thundering rocket blasts, the glassite dome of Kahora, Trade City for Mars, rose jewel-like out of the red sand. The little sun stared wearily down and the ancient hills considered it, and the old, old wandering wind passed over it, and it seemed as though the planet bore Kahora and its spaceport with

7

patience, as though it were a small local infection that would soon be gone.

He had forgotten Johnny Niles. He had forgotten everything but his own dark thoughts. The young officer studied him with covert pity, and he did not know it.

Burk Winters was a big man, and a tough man, tempered by years of deep-space flying. The same glare of naked light that had burned his skin so dark had bleached his hair until it was almost white, and just in the last few months his gray eyes seemed to have caught and held a spark of that pitiless radiance. The easy good nature was gone out of them, and the lines that laughter had shaped around his mouth had deepened now into bitter scars.

A big man, a hard man, but a man who was no longer in control of himself. All during the voyage out from Earth he had chain-smoked the little Venusian cigarettes that have a sedative effect. He was smoking one now, and even so he could not keep his hands steady nor stop the everlasting tic in his right cheek.

"Burk." Johnny's voice came to him from a great distance. "Burk, it's none of my business, but . . ." He hesitated, then blurted out, "Do you think Mars is good for you, now?"

Quite abruptly, Winters said, "Take good care of the *Starflight*, Johnny. Goodbye."

He went away, down the ramp. The pilot stared after him.

The Second Officer came up to Johnny. "That guy has sure gone to pieces," he said.

Johnny nodded. He was angry, because he had come up under Winters and he loved him.

"The damn fool," he said. "He shouldn't have come here." He looked out over the mocking immensity of Mars and added, "His girl was lost out there, somewhere. They never found her body."

A spaceport taxi took Burk Winters into Kahora, and Mars vanished. He was back in the world of the Trade Cities, which belong to all planets, and none.

Vhia on Venus, N'York on Earth, Sun City in Mercury's Twilight Belt, the glassite refuges of the Outer Worlds, they were all alike. They were dedicated to the coddling of wealth and greed, little paradises where millions were made

8

and lost in comfort, where men and women from all over the Solar System could expend their feverish energies without regard for such annoyances as weather and gravitation.

Other things than the making of money were done in the Trade Cities. The lovely plastic buildings, the terraces and gardens and the glowing web of moving walks that spun them together, offered every pleasure and civilized vice of the known worlds.

Winters hated the Trade Cities. He was used to the elemental honesty of space. Here the speech, the dress, even the air one breathed, were artificial.

And he had a deeper reason than that for his hatred.

Yet he had left N'York in feverish haste to reach Kahora, and now that he was here he felt that he could not endure even the delay caused by the necessity of crossing the city. He sat tensely on the edge of the seat, and his nervous twitching grew worse by the minute.

When finally he reached his destination, he could not hold the money for his fare. He dropped the plastic tokens on the floor and left the driver to scramble for them.

He stood for a moment, looking up at the ivory façade before him. It was perfectly plain, the epitome of expensive unpretentiousness. Above the door, in small letters of greenish silver, was the one Martian word: *Shanga.*

"The return," he translated. "The going-back." A strange and rather terrible smile crossed his face, very briefly. Then he opened the door and went inside.

Subdued lighting, comfortable lounges, soft music, the perfect waiting room. There were half a dozen men and women there, all Terrans. They wore the fashionably simple white tunic of the Trade Cities, which set off the magnificent blaze of their jewelry and the exotic styles in which they dressed their hair.

Their faces were pallid and effeminate, scored with the haggard marks of life lived under the driving tension of a super-modern age.

A Martian woman sat in an alcove, behind a glassite desk. She was dark, sophisticatedly lovely. Her costume was the artfully adapted short robe of ancient Mars, and she wore no ornament. Her slanting topaz eyes regarded Burk Winters with professional pleasantness, but deep in them he could see the scorn and the pride of a race so old that the Terran exquisites of the Trade Cities were only crude children beside it.

"Captain Winters," she said. "How nice to see you again."

He was in no mood for conventional pleasantries. "I want to see Kor Hal," he said. "Now."

"I'm afraid . . ." she began. Then she took another look at Winters' face and turned to the intercom. Presently she said, "You may go in."

He pushed open the door that led into the interior of the building, which consisted almost entirely of a huge solarium. Glassite walls enclosed it. Around the sides were many small cells, containing only a padded table. The roofs of the cells were quartz, and acted as mammoth lenses.

Skirting the solarium on the way to Kor Hal's office, Winters' mouth twisted with contempt as he looked through the transparent wall.

An exotic forest blossomed there. Trees, ferns, brilliant flowers, soft green sward, a myriad of birds. And through this mock-primitive playground wandered the men and women who were devotees of Shanga.

They lay first on the padded tables and let the radiation play with them. Winters knew. Neuro-psychic therapy, the doctors called it. Heritage of the lost wisdom of old Mars. Specific for the jangled nerves and overwrought emotions of modern man, who lived too fast in too complex an environment.

You lie there and the radiation tingles through you. Your glandular balance tips a little. Your brain slows down. All sorts of strange and pleasant things happen inside of you, while the radiation tinkers with nerves and reflexes and metabolism. And pretty soon you're a child again, in an evolutionary sort of way.

Shanga, the going-back. Mentally, and just a tiny bit physically, back to the primitive, until the effect wore off and the normal balance restored itself. And even then, for a while, you felt better and happier, because you'd had one hell of a rest, from everything.

Their pampered white bodies incongruously clad in skins and bits of colored cloth, the Earthlings of Kahora played and fought among the trees, and their worries were simple

10

ones concerning food and love and strings of gaudy beads.

Hidden away out of sight were watchful men with shock guns. Sometimes someone went a little bit too far down the road. Winters knew. He had been knocked cold himself, on his last visit here. He remembered that he had tried to kill a man.

Or rather, he had been told that he had tried to kill a man. One did not remember much of the interludes of Shanga. That was one reason people liked it. One was free of inhibitions.

Fashionable vice, made respectable by the cloak of science. It was a new kind of excitement, a new kind of escape from the glittering complexities of life. The Terrans were mad for it.

But only the Terrans. The barbaric Venusians were still too close to the savage to have any need for it, and the Martians were too old and wise in sin to use it. *Besides,* thought Winters, *they made Shanga. They know.*

A deep shudder ran through him as he thrust his way into the office of Kor Hal, the director.

Kor Hal was lean and dark and of no particular age. His national origin was lost in the anonymity of the conventional white tunic. He was Martian, and his courtesy was only a velvet sheath over chilled steel, but beyond that he was quantity X.

"Captain Winters," he said. "Please sit down."

Winters sat.

Kor Hal studied him. "You're nervous, Captain Winters. But I am afraid to treat you anymore. Atavism lies too close to the surface in you." He shrugged. "You remember the last time."

Winters nodded. "The same thing happened in N'York." He leaned forward. "I don't want you to treat me anymore. What you have here isn't enough now. Sar Kree told me that, in N'York. He told me to come to Mars."

Kor Hal said quietly, "He communicated with me."

"Then you will . . ." Winters broke off, because there were no words with which to finish his question.

Kor Hal did not answer. He reclined at ease against the cushions of his lounge chair, handsome, unconcerned. Only his eyes, which were green and feral, held a buried spark

11

of amusement. The cruel amusement of a cat which has a crippled mouse under its paw.

"Are you sure," he asked finally, "that you know what you're doing?"

"Yes."

"People differ, Captain Winters. Those mannikins out there" —he indicated the solarium—"have neither blood nor heart. They are artificial products of an artificial environment. But men like you, Winters, are playing with fire when they play with Shanga."

"Listen," said Winters. "The girl I was going to marry took her flier out over the desert one day and never came back. God only knows what happened to her. You know better than I do the things that can happen to people in the dead sea bottoms. I hunted for her. I found her flier, where it had crashed. I never found her. After that nothing mattered much to me. Nothing but forgetting."

Kor Hal inclined his dark, narrow head. "I remember. A tragedy, Captain Winters. I knew Miss Leland, a lovely young woman. She used to come here."

"I know," said Winters. "She wasn't Trade City, really, but she had too much money and too much time. Anyway, I'm not worried about playing with your fire, Kor Hal. I've been burned too deep with it already. Like you say, people differ. Those lily-whites in their toy jungle, they have no desire to go back any farther. They haven't the guts or the passions to want to. I have."

Winters' eyes blazed with a peculiarly animal light. "I want to go back, Kor Hal. Back as far as Shanga will take me."

"Sometimes," said the Martian, "that's a long way."

"I don't care."

Kor Hal gave him an intent look. "For some, there is no return."

"I have nothing to return to."

"It is not easy, Winters. Shanga—the real Shanga, of which these solariums and quartz lenses are only a weak copy, was forbidden centuries ago by the City-States of Mars. There are risks, and discomforts, which means that the process is expensive."

"I have money." Winters leaped up suddenly, his control breaking. "Be damned to your arguments! They're all hypocrisy, anyway. You know perfectly well which ones are going to take to Shanga. You keep them coming until they're addicts, half crazy to feel the real thing, and you know damn well you're going to give them what they want as soon as they cross your dirty palm with silver."

He tossed a checkbook on Kor Hal's desk. The top one was blank, but signed.

"There," he said. "Anything up to a hundred-thousand Universal Credits."

"I would prefer," said Kor Hal, "that you draw your own check, to cash." He handed the checkbook back to Winters. "The full amount, in advance."

Burk Winters said one word. "When?"

"Tonight, if you wish. Where are you staying?"

"The Tri-Planet."

"Have dinner there as usual. Then remain in the bar. Sometime during the evening your guide will join you."

"I'll be waiting," Winters said, and went out.

Kor Hal smiled. His teeth were very white, very sharp. They had the hungry look of fangs.

II

BURK WINTERS got his bearings finally when Phobos rose, and he could guess where they were heading.

They had slipped quietly out of Kahora, he and the slender young Martian who had joined him unobtrusively in the Tri-Planet bar. A flier waited for them on a private field. Kor Hal waited also. They took off, with a fourth man, who looked to be one of the big barbarians from the northern hills of Kesh. Kor Hal took the controls.

Winters was sure now that they were bound for the Low Canals, the ancient waterways and the ancient wicked towns —Jekkara, Valkis, Barrakesh—outside the laws of the scattered City-States. Thieves' market, slave market, vice market of a world. Earthmen were warned to keep away from them.

Miles reeled behind them. The utter desolation of the landscape below got on Winters' nerves. The silence in the

13

flier became unendurable. There was something menacing about it. Kor Hal and the big Keshi and the slim young man seemed to be nursing some common inner thought that gave them a peculiarly vicious pleasure. Its shadow showed on their faces.

Winters spoke finally. "Are your headquarters out here?" No answer.

Winters said rather petulantly, "There's no need to be so secretive. After all, I'm one of you now."

The slim young man said sharply, "Do the beasts lie down with the masters?"

Winters started to bristle, and the barbarian put his hand on the wicked little sap he carried at his belt. Then Kor Hal spoke coolly.

"You wished to practice Shanga in its true form, Captain Winters. That is what you have paid for. That is what you will receive. All else is irrelevant."

Winters shrugged sulkily. He sat smoking his sedative tobacco, and he did not speak again.

After a long, long time the seemingly endless desert began to change. Low ridges rose naked from the sand and grew into a mountain range, of which nothing was left now but the barren rock.

Beyond the mountains lay a dead sea bottom. It stretched away under the moonlight, dropping, always dropping, until at last it became only a vast pit of darkness. Ribs of chalk and coral gleamed here and there, pushing through the lichens like bones through the dried skin of a man long dead.

Winters saw that there was a city between the foothills and the sea.

It had followed the receding water down the slopes. From this height, Winters could see the outlines of five harbors, abandoned one by one as the sea drew back, the great stone docks still standing. Houses had been built to fill their emptiness, and then abandoned in their turn for a lower level.

Now the straggling town had coalesced along the bank of the canal that drew what feeble life was left from the buried springs of the bottom. There was something infinitely

14

sad about that thin dark line—all that was left of a blue and rolling ocean.

The flier circled and came down. The Keshi said something rapidly in his own dialect, from which Winters caught the one word, *Valkis*. Kor Hal answered him. Then he turned to Winters and said:

"We have not far to go. Stay close by me."

The four men left the flier. Winters knew that he was under guard, and felt that it was not entirely for the sake of protecting him.

The wind blew thin and dry. Dust rose in clouds around their feet. Valkis lay ahead, a stony darkness sprawling upward toward the cliffs, cold in the eerie light of the twin moons. Winters saw, high up on the crest, the broken towers of a palace.

They walked beside still black water, on paving stones worn hollow by the sandaled feet of countless generations. Even at this late hour, Valkis did not sleep. Torches burned yellow against the night. Somewhere a double-banked harp made strange music. The streets, the alley mouths, the doorways and the flat roofs of the houses rustled with life.

Lithe lean men and catlike women watched the strangers, hot-eyed and silent. And over all, Winters heard the particular sound of the Low Canal towns—the whispering and chiming of the wanton little bells that the women wear, braided into their dark hair, hanging from their ears, chained around their ankles.

Evil, that town. Ancient, and very evil, but not tired. Winters could feel the pulse of life that beat there, strong and hot. He was afraid. His own civilian garb and the white tunics of his companions were terribly conspicuous in this place of bare breasts and bright kilts and jeweled girdles.

No one molested them. Kor Hal led the way into a large house and shut the door of beaten bronze behind them, and Winters felt a great relief. He turned to Kor Hal.

"How soon?" he asked, and tried to conceal the trembling of his hands.

"Everything is ready, Winters. Halk, show him the way."

The Keshi nodded and went off, with Winters at his heels. This was very different from the Hall of Shanga in Kahora.

15

Within these walls of quarried stone, men and women had lived and loved and died in violence. The blood and tears of centuries had dried in the cracks between the flags. The rugs, the tapestries, and the furnishings were worth a fortune as antiques. Their beauty was worn, but still bright.

At the end of a corridor was a bronze door, pierced by a narrow grille.

Halk stopped. He said to Winters, "Strip."

Winters hesitated. He carried a gun, and he did not like to leave it behind. "Why out here? I'd rather have my clothes with me."

Halk said, "Strip here. It is the rule."

Winters obeyed.

He walked naked into the narrow cell. There was no comfortable table here, only a few skins thrown on the bare floor. A barred opening showed darkly in the opposite wall.

The bronze door rang shut behind him and he heard the great bar drop into place. It was completely dark. He was really afraid, now. Terribly afraid. But it was too late for that. It had been too late, for a long time.

Ever since Jill Leland was lost.

He lay down on the hides. High above, in the vault of the roof, he could make out a faint, vague shimmering. It grew brighter. Presently he saw that it was a prism set into the stone, rather large and cut from a crystalline substance that was the color of fire.

Kor Hal's voice reached him through the grille. "Earthman!"

"Yes?"

"That prism is one of the Jewels of Shanga. The wise men of Caer Dhu carved them half a million years ago. Only they knew the secret of the substance, and the shaping of the facets. There are only three of the jewels left."

Sparks that were more energy than light flickered on the stone walls of the cell. Gold and orange and greenish blue. Little flames, the fire of Shanga, to burn the heart.

Because he was afraid, Winters said, "But the radiation, the ray that comes through the prism. Is it the same as that in Kahora?"

"Yes. The secret of the projectors was lost also with Caer

Dhu. Presumably they use cosmic rays. By substituting ordinary quartz for the prisms, we could make the radiation weak enough for our purpose in the Trade Cities."

"Who is 'we,' Kor Hal?"

Laughter, soft and wicked. "Earthman—we are Mars!"

Dancing fire, growing, growing, glinting on his flesh, darting through his blood, his brain. It was not like this in the solariums, with their pretty trees. It was pleasure there, tantalizing, heady pleasure. It was exciting, and strange. But this . . .

His body began to move, to arch itself into strong writhing curves. He thought he could not endure the lovely, lovely pain.

Kor Hal's voice boomed down some huge fateful distance. "The wise men of Caer Dhu were not so wise. They found the secret of Shanga, and they escaped their wars and their troubles by fleeing backward along the path of evolution. Do you know what happened to them? They perished, Earthman! In one generation, Caer Dhu vanished from the face of Mars." It was getting hard to answer, hard to think. Winters said hoarsely, "Did it matter? They were happy, while they lived."

"Are you happy, Earthman?"

"Yes!" he panted. "Yes!"

The words were only half articulate. Twisting, rolling on the hide rugs, in the grip of such magnificent, unholy sensation as he had never dreamed of before, Burk Winters was happy. The fire of Shanga blazed down upon him like a melting away, and there was nothing left but joy.

Again, Kor Hal laughed.

After that, Winters was not sure of anything. His mind rocked, and there were periods of darkness. When he was conscious, he knew only a feeling of *strangeness*. But he carried one memory with him, at least part way down that eerie road.

During a lucid period, a space of only a minute or two, he thought that one of the stones had rolled back to reveal a quartzite screen, and that through the screen a face looked at him, watching as he bathed naked in the beautiful flame.

A woman's face. Martian, highbred, with strong delicate

17

bones and arrogant brows, and a red mouth that would be like a bittersweet fruit to kiss. Her eyes were golden as the fire, and as hot, and proud, and scornful.

There must have been a microphone in the wall, for she spoke and he heard her voice, full of a sweet cruel magic. She called his name. He could not rise, but he managed to crawl toward her, and to his reeling brain she was part of the unearthly force that played with him. A destruction and a fascination, as irresistible as death.

To his alien eyes, she was not as lovely as Jill. But there was a power in her. And her red mouth taunted him, and the curve of her bare shoulders drove him to madness.

"You're strong," she said. "You will live, until the end. And that is well, Burk Winters."

He tried to speak, but he could no longer form the words.

She smiled. "You have challenged me, Earthman. I know. You've challenged Shanga. You're brave, and I like brave men. You're also a fool, and I like fools, because they give me sport. I'm looking forward, Earthman, to the moment when you reach the end of your search!"

He tried again to speak, and failed, and then the night and the silence came to stay. He took the sound of her mocking laughter with him into the dark.

He did not think of himself now as Captain Burk Winters, but only by the short personal name of Burk. The stones upon which he lay were cold and hard. It was pitch-dark, but his eyes and ears were very keen. He could tell by the sound of his breathing that he was in a closed space, and he did not like it.

A low growl rumbled in his throat. The hairs stiffened at the back of his neck. He tried to remember how he had come here. Something had happened, something to do with fire, but he did not know what, or why.

Only one thing he knew. He was searching for something. It was gone, and he wanted it back. The wanting was a pain in him. He could not remember what the object was that he wanted, but the need for it was greater than any obstacle short of death.

He rose and began to explore his prison.

Almost at once he found an opening. Cautious testing told him that there was a passage beyond. He could see nothing, but the air that blew in to him was very heavy with strange smells. Instinct told him that it was a trap. He crouched resolute, his hands opening and closing in desire for a weapon. There was no weapon. Presently he went into the passage, moving without sound.

He went a long way, his shoulders brushing stone on either side. Then he saw light ahead, red and flickering, and the air brought him the taint of smoke, and the smell of man.

Very, very slowly, the creature called Burk padded toward the light.

He came close to the end of the tunnel, and suddenly a barred gate dropped behind him with a ringing clash. He could not go back.

He did not wish to go back. Enemies were in front of him, and he wished to fight. He knew now that he could not come upon them secretly. Flexing his great chest, he leaped out boldly from the tunnel mouth.

The tossing glare of torches dazzled his eyes, and a wild mob howl deafened him. He stood alone on a great block—the old slave block of Valkis, though he did not know that. They stared up, jeering at the Earthman who had tasted the forbidden fruit that even the soulless men of the Low Canals would not touch.

The creature called Burk was still a man, but a man already shadowed by the ape. During the hours he had bathed in the light of Shanga, he had changed physically. Bone and flesh had altered under the accelerated urging of glands and increased metabolism.

Already a big, powerful man, he had thickened and coarsened along the lines of brutish strength. His jaw and brow ridges jutted. Thick hair covered his chest and limbs and extended in a rudimentary mane down the back of his neck. His deep-set eyes had a hard and cunning gleam of intelligence, but it was the intelligence of the primitive mind that had learned to speak and make fire and weapons, and no more than that.

Half crouching, he glared down at the crowd. He did not know who these men were; he hated them. They were

19

of another tribe, and their very smell was alien. They hated him, too. The air bristled with their enmity.

His gaze fell on a man who stepped out lightly and proudly into the empty space. He did not remember that this man's name was Kor Hal. He did not notice that Kor Hal had shed the white tunic of the Trade Cities for the kilt and girdle of the Low Canals, nor that he wore in his ears the pierced gold rings of Barrakesh, and was now honestly himself—a bandit, born and bred among a race of bandits who had been civilized for so long that they could afford to forget it.

Burk knew only that this man was his particular enemy.

"Captain Burk Winters," said Kor Hal. "Man of the tribe of Terra—lords of the spaceways, builders of the Trade Cities, masters of greed and rapine."

His voice carried over the packed square, though he did not shout. Burk watched him, his eyes like blinking red sparks in the torchlight, weaving slightly on his feet, his hands swinging loose and hungry. He did not understand the words, but they were threat and insult.

"Look at him, Oh men of Valkis!" cried Kor Hal. "He is our master now. His government kings it over the City-States of Mars. Our pride is stripped, our wealth is gone. What have we left, oh children of a dying world?"

The answer that rang from the walls of Valkis was soft and wordless, the opening chord of a hymn written in hell.

Someone threw a stone.

Burk came down off the slave block in a great effortless spring and sped across the square, straight for Kor Hal's throat.

A laugh went up, mirth that was half a cat-scream of sheer savagery. Like one supple creature, the crowd moved. Torchlight flashed from knife-blades and jewels and eyes of glittering green and topaz, and the small chiming bells, and the points of the deadly spiked knuckle-dusters. Long black tongues of whips licked out with a hiss and a crack.

Kor Hal waited until Burk almost reached him. Then he bent and pivoted in the graceful Martian savatte. His foot caught Burk under the chin and sent him sprawling.

As he rolled half stunned, Kor Hal caught a whip from a man's hand.

"That's it, Earthman!" he cried out. "Grovel! Belly down, and lick the stones that were here before the apes of Earth had learned to walk!"

The long lash sang and bit, lacing the hairy body with red weals, and the harsh mob scream went up—*Drive him! Drive the beast of Shanga, as the invading beasts of old were driven by our forefathers!*"

And they drove him, with whip and knife and spike, through the streets of Valkis under the racing moons. Jeering, they drove him.

He fought them. Mad with fury, he fought them, but he could not come to grips with them. When he lunged they melted before him, and each way he turned he was met by the lash and the blade and the crippling kick. Blood ran, but it was all his own, and the high shrill laughter of women pursued him as he went.

He wanted to kill. The lust of killing was more red and strong within him than his blood. But he reeled under the pain of many blows, and his sight was dim, and where his great hands closed on flesh to tear it, he was himself torn and driven back, dragged down by the lashes curled around his throat.

At last there was only fear and the desire to escape.

They let him run. Along the crumbling ways of Valkis, up and down the twisting alleys that reeked of ancient crime, they let him run. But not too far. They blocked him off from the canal and the freedom of the sea bottom beyond. Again and again they headed the panting, shambling creature that had been Burk Winters, captain of the *Starflight*, and drove it higher up the slope.

Burk moved slowly now. He snarled and his head wove blindly from side to side in a pathetic attempt at defiance. His blood dripped hot on the stones. And always the insolent stinging lashes drove him on.

Up and up. Past the great looming docks, with the bollards and the scars of moored ships still on them, and the dust of their own decay lapping dry around their feet. Four levels above the canal. Four harbors, four cities, four epochs written in fading characters of stone. Even the dawn-man Burk was oppressed and frightened.

There was no life here. There had been no life for a long

21

time, even in the lowest level. The wind had scoured and polished the empty houses, smoothing the corners to roundness, hollowing the doors and windows, until the work of man was almost erased. Only strange things were left, that looked as though the wind had made them by itself out of little mountain tops.

The people of Valkis were silent now. They drove the beast, and their hate had not abated, but was intensified.

They walked here upon the very bones of their world. Earth was a green star, young and rich. Here the Martians passed the marble pier where the Kings of Valkis had moored their galleys, and the very marble was shattered under the heel of time.

High on the ridge above the oldest city the palace of the kings looked down at the scourging of the interloper. And in all of Valkis now there was no sound but the whispering of little bells that was like the sigh of wind on another world, where the women ran on their small bare feet, ankle deep in dust.

Burk climbed apelike up the history of Mars. His belly was cold with a terror of these dark places that smelled of nothing, not even of death.

He passed a place where houses had been built within the curve of a coral reef. He clambered over the reef, and saw above him a sloping face of rock with gaping holes that the sea had made. He climbed that, not knowing or caring what it was.

On the level space above he passed the broken quays that had once made safe mooring in the bay, and stopped to look back.

They were still hunting him. His flanks heaved and his eyes were desperate. He went on, scrambling up steep narrow streets where the paving blocks had fallen out and the houses had come down in shapeless heaps, and his hands and feet left red prints where he put them down.

Then, at last, he was at the top of the ridge.

The great bulk of the palace loomed above him against the sky. Primitive wisdom told him the place was dangerous. He skirted the high wall of marble that ringed it, and suddenly his twitching nostrils caught the scent of water.

His tongue was swollen in his mouth, his throat choked

with dust. His need was so great, with the salt bleeding and the fever of his wounds, that he forgot his enemies and the menace of the mountain-thing behind the wall. Breaking into a ragged lope, he went forward along the cliff top until he came to a gateway, and plunged through it, and suddenly there was turf under his feet, soft and cool. There were shrubs, and flowers pale in the moonlight, heavily sweet, and dark branches against the sky.

The gate closed silently behind him. He did not see it. He ran down a grassy ride between rows of trees trimmed into fantastic shapes, guided by the smell of water. Here and there were strange gleams and glints of statuary, wrought in marble and semiprecious stones. Burk's skin crawled with an awareness of danger, but he was too weary and too mad with thirst to care.

The ride ended. Beyond was an open space, and in the center of it was a great sunken tank, carved and ornamented. The water in it was like polished jet.

Nothing stirred in the open. A wing of the place rose beyond the tank like a black wall, and it seemed that nothing lived there, but Burk's hair-trigger nerves told him otherwise. He stopped in the shelter of the trees, sniffing the air and listening.

Nothing. Darkness and silence. Burk looked at the waiting water. It filled all his senses. Suddenly he ran toward it.

He flung himself belly down on the slabs of turquoise that paved the brink and buried his face in the icy water and drank. Then he lay there panting, utterly spent.

Still nothing moved.

Then, all at once, a long howl rose on the night, from somewhere beyond the palace wing. Burk stiffened. He got to his hands and knees, every hair on his body bristling with fear.

The howl was answered by a strange reptilian scream.

Now that he had satisfied his thirst, the night wind brought him many odors. They were too numerous and tangled to be identified, except for a strong musky taint that made his flesh crawl with instinctive loathing. He did not know what sort of creature gave off that taint, but it filled him with horror, because it seemed that he *almost knew*—and did not want to.

He wanted only to get away from that place, that was so full of secret life and hidden menace and silence.

He began to move toward the trees, back the way he had come. Slowly, because he was wounded and very weak. And then, quite suddenly, he saw her.

She had come without sound into the open space, out of the shelter of huge flowering shrubs. She stood not far away, in the shifting glow of the little racing moons, watching him. She was shy and large-eyed, poised for flight. The hair that hung down her back and the shining down that covered her body were the color of the moonlight.

Burk stopped. A tremor went through him. All his sense of loss and his desperate searching came back to him, and with them a desire to be closer to this slender she.

A name spoke itself from some dim chamber of his soul. "Jill?"

She started. He thought she was going to run away, and he cried out again, "Jill!" Then, step by step, uncertainly, she came nearer, lovely as a fawn in spring.

She made a questioning sound, and he answered. "Burk." She stood still for a moment, repeating the word, and then she whimpered and began to run toward him, and he was filled with a great joy. He laughed and mouthed her name over and over, and there were tears in his eyes. He reached out toward her.

A spear flashed and fell quivering between them.

She gave him a cry of warning and fled, vanishing into the shrubbery. Burk tried to follow, but his knees gave under him. He turned, snarling.

Tall Keshi guards in resplendent harness had come out of the trees, circling behind him. They carried spears and a net of heavy ropes. In a moment he was surrounded. The spear-points pricked him back until the net was thrown, and he went down helpless.

As they carried him away, he heard two things. The wail of the silver she, and from somewhere nearby, a woman's mocking laughter.

He had heard that laughter before. He could not remember where, or how, but it filled him with such fury that he was finally knocked over the head with a spear-butt, to keep him quiet.

III

HE CAME to himself—the self that was Captain Burk Winters —in a room that was much like the one he last remembered, in Valkis, except that the walls were of a dark green rock and there was no prism.

Winters could not remember anything of what had happened since that last room, except that he knew he had had a strong emotional shock. Jill's name was uppermost in his mind. He began to tremble with a deep excitement.

He got to his feet, and it was then that he realized he was shackled. Chains ran from cuffs on his wrists to similar cuffs on his ankles, passing through rings on a metal belt around his waist. These constituted his entire clothing. He saw also that there were freshly healed scars on his body.

The heavy door was opened for him before he could begin to pound on it. Four tall barbarians, their harness magnificent with jewels and wrought metal, formed up a guard around him, and an officer led the way. They did not speak to Winters, and he knew the uselessness of trying to get anything out of them.

He had not the faintest idea where he was, or how he had come there, beyond a vague memory of pain and flight that was like something he had dreamed.

And somewhere, during that dream, he had seen Jill, spoken to her. He was as certain of that as he was of the weight of his chains.

He stumbled, because his sight was blurred with tears. Up to then, he had not been sure. He had seen the twisted wreck of her flier, and while he did not believe it, there was always the chance that she might really be dead, and lost to him beyond all hope.

Now he knew. She was alive, and if Winters had been alone he would have wept like a child.

Instead, he studied the corridors and the great halls through which the guard took him. From the size and the splendor of them he knew that he was in a palace, and guessed that it might be the one he had seen on the cliffs above Valkis. This was confirmed when he caught a glimpse of the town through a window embrasure.

The palace was older than anything he had seen on Mars, except for the buried ruins of Lhak in the northern deserts. But this was no ruin. It had grown old in somber beauty. The patterns of the mosaic floors were blurred, the precious stones worn thin as porcelain. The tapestries, preserved by the wonderful Martian formula that had been lost for centuries, like everything else on Mars, had grown frail and brittle, their colors all softened to faint glows, infinitely sad and lovely.

Here and there, on the walls or the soaring vault of a roof, were murals—magnificent pageants of lost glory, dim as an old man's memory. The seas they pictured were deep and blue, and the ships were tall, and the mail of the warriors was set with gems, and the captive queens were beautiful as dusky pearls.

Proud architecture, mating beauty with strength, and showing that strange blend of culture and barbarism that is so typically Martian. Winters reflected on how long ago these stones had been quarried, and went on to reflect that at that time civilization had already destroyed itself in a series of atomic wars, and the proud Kings of Valkis were only bandit chieftains in a world that was slipping downward toward the night.

They came at length to doors of beaten gold that were more than twice Burk's six-foot height. The Keshi guards who stood there pushed them wide, and Burk saw the throne room.

Westering sunlight slanted in from the high embrasures, falling across the pillars and the tesselated floor. The pale light touched vagrant glints from the shields and the weapons of dead kings, warmed the old banners to brief life. Everywhere else in that vast place was a brooding darkness, full of whispers and small faint echoings.

A shaft of cool gold fell directly upon the throne at the far end of the room.

The high seat itself was cut from a single block of black basalt, and as Winters approached it, his swinging chains making a loud sound in the silence, he saw that the stone had been already half shaped by the sea. It was very worn

26

and smooth with the patient sanding of the tides, and where hands had lain on the armpieces there were deep hollows, and on the basalt step below.

An old woman sat upon the throne. She was wrapped in a black cloak, and her hair wound into a sort of white crown on her head, braided with jewels. She stared with half-blind eyes at the Earthman, and suddenly she spoke, in sonorous High Martian, a tongue as antique on Mars as Sanskrit is on Earth. Winters could not understand one word of it, but he knew from her tone and expression that she was quite mad.

Someone sat in the heavy shadows by her feet, outside the shaft of sunlight, and veiled by it from Winters' sight. He could catch only a vague pallor of ivory-tinted flesh, but for some reason his nerves tingled with premonition.

As he neared the high seat, the old woman rose and stretched out her arm toward him, a wrinkled Cassandra crying doom upon his head. The wild echoes of her voice rolled from the vaulted roof, and her eyes were full of a blazing hate.

The guards set the butts of their spears into his back so that he was thrown face down before the basalt step. A low, sweet, mocking laugh came out of the shadows, and he felt the pressure of a little sandaled foot on his neck.

He knew the voice that said, "Greeting, Captain Winters! The throne of Valkis welcomes you."

The foot was withdrawn from his neck. He rose. The old woman had fallen back onto the throne. She was intoning what sounded like a church litany, and her upturned face had an exalted look.

The remembered voice said out of the dimness, "My mother is repeating the coronation rites. Presently she will demand the year's tribute from the Outer Islands and the coastal tribes. Time and reality do not bother her, and it pleases her to play at being queen. Therefore, as you see, I, Fand, rule Valkis from the shadow of the throne."

"Sometimes," Winters said, "you must come into the light."

"Yes."

A soft, quick rustle and she was standing there in the shaft of sunlight. Her hair was the color of night after moonset, intricately coiled. She was dressed in the old, arrogant fashion of the bandit kingdoms—the long full skirt slit to the waist at the sides, so that her thighs showed when she moved, the wide jeweled girdle, collar of golden plaques. Her small, high breasts were bare and lovely, her body slender, with a catlike grace.

Her face was as he remembered it. Proud and fine, golden-eyed, a mouth like a red fruit that mingled honey and poison, a lazy, slumbrous power behind the beauty, the fascination of all things that are at once beautiful and deadly.

She looked at Winters and smiled. "So at last you have reached the end of your search."

He looked down at his chains and his nakedness. "A strange way to reach it. I paid Kor Hal well for this privilege." He gave her a searching glance. "Do you rule Shanga, as well as Valkis? If so you're not very courteous to your guests."

"On the contrary, I treat them very well—as you shall see." Her golden eyes taunted him. "But you didn't come here to practice Shanga, Captain Winters."

"Why else would I have come?"

"To find Jill Leland."

He was not really surprised. Subconsciously he had known that she knew. But he managed a look of blank amazement.

"Jill Leland is dead."

"Was she, when you saw her in the garden, and spoke to her?" Fand laughed. "Do you think we're such fools? Everyone who comes to the Hall of Shanga in the Trade Cities is carefully checked and examined. We were particularly careful with you, Captain Winters, because psychologically you were the wrong type to be drawn to Shanga. Men like you are too strong to need escape.

"You knew, of course, that your fiancée had taken up the practice. You didn't like it, and tried to make her stop. Kor Hal said that she was terribly upset about it on several occasions. But Jill had gone too far to stop. She begged to be allowed the full power, the real Shanga. She helped us plan her supposed death in the sea bottom. We would have done that anyway, for our own protection, since the girl has influential connections and we can't afford to have people hunting for our clients. But she wanted you to believe that she was dead, so that you would forget her. She felt she had no right to marry you, that she would ruin your life. Doesn't that touch you, Captain Winters? Doesn't that bring tears to your eyes?"

It brought more than that to Winters. It brought an overpowering urge to take this lovely she-devil between his hands and break her and then stamp the pieces into the earth.

His chains made one harsh jangling sound, and then the spears came up and touched his flesh with sharp red kisses. He stood still and said, "Why have you done this? Is it for money, or for hate?"

"For both, Earthman! And for something more important than either of them." Her lips curved in brief amusement. "Besides, I've done nothing to your people. I built the Halls of Shanga, yes. But the men and women of Earth degrade themselves of their own free will. Come here."

She motioned him to follow her to the window. As she crossed the vast room, she said, "You have seen part of the palace. Earth credits have rebuilt and restored the house of my fathers. The credits of apelings who wish to return to their normal state because the civilization they have forced themselves is too much for them. Look out there. Earth money has done that, too."

Winters looked out upon a sight that had almost vanished from the face of Mars. A garden, the varied and jewel-bright garden that would have belonged with a palace like this. Broad lawns of bronze green turf, formal plantings, statuary . . .

For some reason he could not quite remember, that garden gave Burk Winters a cold shuddering chill.

But the garden itself was only a part of what he saw. A small part. Beneath the window the ground sloped away into a vast bowl-shaped depression, perhaps a quarter-mile away, and Winters looked down into an amphitheater. Ruined as it was, it was still magnificent, with tiers of seats rising like steps of hewn stone from the inner walls. He thought of how it must have looked when the games were held in the old days, with all of those thousands of places filled.

Now, in the arena, there was another garden. A wild and

tangled garden, closed in by the high protective walls that had kept the beasts from the spectators. There were trees in it, and open spaces, and he could make out moving forms among the shadows, strange forms. He could not see them clearly for the distance and the slanting light, but a chill pang struck through him, a cold breath of foreboding.

In the center of the arena was a lake. Not a large one, and probably not deep, but there were creatures splashing in it, and he caught the faint echo of a reptilian scream. An echo he had heard before. . . .

Fand was looking outward to the amphitheater, with an odd, slow smile. Winters saw that there were people already in the lower tiers of the seats, and more of them gathering.

"What is this thing," he asked her, "that is more important than money or your hatred for the men of Earth?"

All the ancient pride of her race and house flashed out in her eyes as she answered him. He forgot his loathing of her for a moment, in his respect for her deep sincerity.

She said only one word. "Mars."

The old woman heard her and cried out from the throne. Then she flung the corner of her black mantel over her head and was silent.

"Mars," said Fand quietly. "The world that could not even die in decency and honor, because the carrion birds came flying to pick its bones, and the greedy rats suck away the last of its blood and pride."

Winters said, "I don't understand. What has Shanga to do with Mars?"

"You'll see." She turned on him suddenly. "You challenged Shanga, Earthman, just as your people have challenged Mars. We'll find out which is the stronger!"

She motioned to the officer of the guard, who went away. Then she said to Winters, "You wanted your girl back. You were willing to go through the fire of Shanga for her, though you abhorred it. You were willing to risk your identity through the changes of the ray—*which after a while, Earthman, never go away.* And all for Jill Leland. Do you still want her back?"

"Yes."

"You're sure of that."

"Yes."

"Very well." Fand glanced over his shoulder and nodded. "There she is."

For a long moment, Burk Winters did not turn around.

Fand moved away a little, watching with a cruel, amused interest. Winters' back stiffened. He turned.

She was there, standing in the sunlight, bewildered, frightened, a wild and shining creature out of the dawn of the world, with a rope around her neck. The guards were laughing.

Winters thought desperately, *She has not changed too much. Back to the primitive, but not yet to the ape. There is a soul still in her eyes, and the light of reason.*

Jill, Jill! How could you have done this thing?

But he understood now how she could have done it. He remembered how bitterly he had quarreled with her over Shanga. He had thought it a stupid and childish thing, far beneath her intelligence and as degrading as any other drug. But he had not understood.

He did now. And he was filled with a deadly fear, because he understood so well.

Because he himself was now numbered among the beasts of Shanga. And beneath his horror as he looked at the creature that was Jill and yet not Jill, he was aware that in some unholy way he found her more beautiful and more alluring than he ever had before. Stripped of all the shams and the studied unconventions of society, freed of all complexity, her body strong and fleet as a doe's quivering with sensitive life . . .

It would take two of a kind. Dawn-woman, dawn-man. Strong sinew, strong passion, the guts that cities stole away . . .

Fand said, "She can still be saved, if you can find a way to do it." Then she added shrewdly, "Unless you now need someone to save *you*, Captain Winters!"

A strong shock of revulsion rocked him, but his eyes still held a strange light.

The silver she was coming toward him. Her gaze was fixed upon him. He saw that she was drawn to him, and struggling to understand why. She did not speak, and somehow Winters' throat closed on an aching lump, so that he too was dumb.

31

The guard who held her rope let her move as she would. She came close to Winters, hesitantly, as an animal does. Then she stopped and looked up into his face. Tears gathered in her wide dark eyes. Presently she whimpered, very softly, and went down on her knees at his feet.

The old woman let out a shrill cackling. Fand's eyes were like cups of molten gold.

Winters bent over and caught Jill in his arms. He lifted her to her feet and stood holding her to him, in a fury of protective possessive love. He said very softly to Fand, "You've seen it all now. Can we go?"

She nodded. "Take them to the garden of Shanga," she said, and added, "It is almost time."

The guards took them, Burk Winters and the woman he had lost and found again, out through the great echoing halls of the palace and down the long slope of lawn to the amphitheater.

A barred gate of heavy metal covered the mouth of a tunnel. The guards unlocked it and took off Winters' chains and thrust him inside with Jill. The gate was locked again behind them.

Holding Jill tightly by the hand, Winters went down the tunnel and came presently into the arena—into the garden of Shanga.

He stopped, blinking in the sudden light. Jill's hand tightened on his. She quivered with a tense expectancy, and her head was tilted in an attitude of listening.

He had only a moment before the gong sounded, the mellow sonorous notes that might have been calling some evil priesthood to its dark prayers. Only a moment to glimpse the trees and the shambling anthropoid forms that moved among them, to catch the rank beast taint in the air, to hear the splashing and the hissing screams from the hidden pool.

Only a moment to be filled with horror and a sick fear, to deny to himself the reality of this nightmare garden, to wish that he were blind and deaf, or better than that, dead.

In the seats above the protecting wall, rows of Martian faces looked down. They were the faces of men and women who watch the antics of creatures in a zoo—destructive creatures for which they have a personal hatred.

Then the gong called out, and Jill leaped away, pulling him by the hand. All over the garden there was a moment of intense silence, and then there rose a devil's chorus of roaring and screaming in voices that were horribly human and even more horribly not, and close to him Jill's voice chimed in, saying over and over, "Shanga! Shanga!"

It came to Winters in a flash, then, what Fand had meant about Mars. As Jill pulled him headlong between the trees and across the open grassy spaces, he realized that this garden of Shanga was in fact a zoo, an exhibit, where the people of Mars might come to see what manner of beast their economic conquerors were. A hot and dire shame rose in him. *Apeling, running naked through the trees, a slave to the fire of Shanga!*

He yelled at Jill to stop!

She only plunged on the harder, so that he had to fight her, setting his heels in the earth. And she turned on him snarling, saying, "Shanga!"

A great anthropoid male came rushing toward them. He had slipped back beyond speech, but ecstatic noises came out of his throat. Behind him were others, males, females, and young on the same evolutionary level. Winters and the silver she that was Jill were caught up and carried on in their tribal rush. Winters fought to get away, but it was hopeless. The wild hairy bodies walled him in.

As they approached the center of the garden they were joined by more and more, all apparently summoned by the sound of the gong. Looking at them, Winters' stomach turned over. This was Walpurgis Night, a festival of blasphemies. And he was trapped in it, inextricably joined to destruction.

The ones like Jill, who had only gone a little way as yet, were not so bad. They were human. Winters knew that he himself had been like that, and he felt no particular horror of them. But there were others. Back through all the stages of the primitive, beyond the Neanderthal, beyond Pithecanthropus Erectus, beyond the missing link, back to the common ancestor.

Shapeless, shambling, hairy brutes, deformed skulls and little red cunning eyes, bared teeth grinning yellow. Things that even the anthropologists had never seen or dreamed

33

of. Things that were not human, or ape, nor any form of life that had ever been classified.

All the dark secrets of Terran evolution were laid bare in this garden, for the Martians to see. It made even Winters, the Earthman, flinch to think that bodies like that had given ultimate birth to him. What respect could the Martians have for such a race, that was still so close to its beginnings?

But he was to see more, much more, of those beginnings. . . .

The gong struck a last booming summons. The tide of bowed hairy shoulders and flat brows and ugly things that went on all fours swept Winters and Jill out into the clearing at the center, where from the palace window he had seen the lake. A strong musky reek hung in the air. It had the same sickly taint that a snake-house does. And Winters saw that the lake was agitated by the creatures who lived there, and who were swarming out to answer the gong.

Back to the common ancestor, and beyond. Beyond the mammal, back to the gill and the scale, to the egg laid in the warm mud, to the hissing, squirming, utterly loathly ultimate!

Jill panted, "Shanga! Shanga!" looking up, and Winters felt a darkness swimming in his brain. A cold wet thing slithered between his legs, and he swayed, retching. The surface of the lake rippled, but he could not look. He could not.

Grasping Jill, he tried to batter his way through the crowd, but it was hopeless. He was caught, trapped.

Looking up, he saw the prisms that were set high overhead on long booms. He saw them start to glow, with the remembered flame.

He had reached the end, now. The end of his search for Jill Leland, the end of everything. The first sweet deadly thrill of the ray touched his flesh. He felt the waking hunger in him, the deep lust, the stirring of the beast that lay so close under his own skin. He thought of the lake, and wondered how it would be to lie in its wetness, breathing through the gill slits that had once opened in his own flesh when he was an embryo in his mother's womb.

Because that is where I shall be, he thought. *In the*

lake. Jill and I. And beyond the lake, what? The amoeba, and then . . . ?

He saw the royal box, whence the Kings of Valkis had watched the gladiators and the flowing blood. Fand sat there now. She leaned her slender elbows on the stone and watched, and it seemed to Winters that even at this distance he could see the smile and the scorn in her golden eyes. Kor Hal sat beside her, and the old woman, a muffled shape of black.

The fires of Shanga burned and brightened. There was a silence on the clearing now. The sounds that came, the moanings and the little whimpers, did not touch the silence. They only made it deeper. The warm glints danced on the upturned faces, glowed in the staring eyes. Each scaled or shaggy body bore a nimbus of beauty. He saw Jill standing there, reaching up toward the twin suns, a slim shaft of silver flame.

The madness already in his blood. Muscle and sinew taut with it, arching, curving. Brain clouding with a bright soft veil, forgetfulness, release. Jill and Burk, dawn-man, dawn-woman, happy while they lived, done with everything but their own love, their own satisfaction. Why not? They were both in it now, both marked with the same stamp.

Then he heard the laughter and the jeering of the Martians who were gathered to watch the shame of his world. He tore his gaze away from the wicked light and looked again into the face of Fand of Valkis, and then at Kor Hal and the thousand other faces, and a bleak and terrible expression came into his eyes.

The ranks of the crowd had broken. The beast-shapes lay upon the turf, writhing in the ecstasy of Shanga. Jill was on her hands and knees. Winters felt the strength going out of him. The lovely pain, the beautiful, wild, exultant pain . . .

He grasped Jill and began to drag her, back toward the trees, out of the circle of light.

She did not want to go. She screamed and tore his face with her nails and kicked him, and he struck her. After that she lay limp in his arms. He kept on, stumbling over the twitching bodies, falling, crawling at last on his hands and knees. Only one thing kept him going on. Only one thing

35

made him undergo the tortures of the damned, fighting Shanga.

That thing was the scornful, smiling face of Fand.

The touch of the ray weakened and was gone. He was safe, beyond the circle. He dragged the girl farther into the shrubbery and turned his back on the clearing because he wanted more than any drug addict could conceive of wanting to go back into the light, and he dared not look at it.

Instead, he pulled himself erect and faced the royal box. It was only pride that kept him standing. He looked straight into the distant eyes of Fand, and her clear silvery voice carried to him.

"You will go back into the fire of Shanga, Earthman. Tomorrow, or the day after—you will go."

Complete assurance there, as one is sure of the rising of the sun.

Burk Winters did not answer. He stood a moment longer, his gaze level with Fand's. Then, even pride failed. He fell and lay still.

The last conscious thought of his mind was that Fand and Mars together had challenged Earth, and that it was no longer merely a matter of saving a girl from destruction.

IV

WHEN HE CAME TO, it was night. Jill sat patiently beside him. She had brought him food, and while he wolfed it down she went away to fetch water in a broad cupped leaf.

He tried to talk to her, but there was a gulf between them too wide to be bridged. She seemed subdued and brooding, and would not come close to him. He had robbed her of the fire of Shanga, and she had not forgotten it.

The futility of trying to escape with her was obvious. After a while he rose and left her, and she did not try to follow.

The garden was still under the light of the low moons. Apparently the beasts of Shanga, true to their ape heritage, were sleeping. Moving with infinite caution, Winters prowled the arena in search of a way out. A plan had taken shape in his mind. It was not much of a plan, and he knew that very probably he would be dead before morning, but he had nothing to lose. He did not even particularly care. He was a man, an Earthman, and there was an anger in him that was deeper than any fear.

The walls of the arena were smooth and high. Even an ape could not have climbed them. All the tunnels were blocked off except the one by which they had entered. He crept down it and found the barred gate impenetrable. Beyond it was a little guard fire, and two sentries.

Winters went back to the arena.

He could see no sign of a guard in the empty tiers of seats. There was no reason for one. In itself, the amphitheater was a perfect prison, and the creatures of the garden had no wish to escape from the besotting joys of Shanga.

Whipped before he started, Winters stood glaring bitterly at the walls that held him fast. Then he caught sight of the booms from which the Shanga prisms were suspended.

Going to the nearest one, he studied it. It was high out of reach, a long metal pole that stretched from the side of the arena above the wall and, with the other one, centered the Shanga-rays over the clearing.

High out of reach. But if a man had a rope . . .

Winters went in among the trees. He found vines and creepers, and tore them away, and knotted them together. He found a small log in a deadfall, big enough to weight one end but light enough for throwing. Then he returned to the boom.

On the third cast the log went over. He drew his flimsy rope down, making a double strand. Hand over hand, praying that the vines would hold, he began to climb.

It seemed like a long way up. He felt very naked and exposed in the moonlight.

The vines held, and no challenging voice shouted at him. He clung to the boom and worked his way along it, first dropping the telltale rope. Presently he was safe among the tiered seats.

Avoiding the guard by the tunnel, he made his way out of the amphitheater and circled out across the slope, keeping to cover where there was cover, crawling on his belly where there was none. The shifting moon-shadows helped him, because they made visibility a treacherous thing. The palace loomed above him, huge and dark, crushed under the weight of time.

Only two lights showed. One, on the ground floor, he guessed would be the guard room. The other, on the third level, was dim as though made by a single torch. That, he hoped, would be the apartment of Fand.

Up the slope and into the shelter of the palace garden, and then into the palace itself. The great half-ruined pile could not have been guarded, even if there had been reason to guard it. Padding silently on naked feet, Winters glided through the vast empty halls, trying to keep a plan of the place straight in his mind.

His eyes were accustomed to the dark, and enough moonlight fell through the embrasures to let him see where he was going. Room and hall and corridor, smelling of dust and death, dreaming over their faded flags and broken trophies, remembering glory. Winters shivered. Something of the cold breath of eternity lived in this place.

He found a ramp, and then another, and at last on the third level he saw light, the weak flicker of it from the crack of a door.

There was no guard. That was a break. Not only because it was a difficulty eliminated, but because it confirmed his guess that Fand was a person who would want no check on her comings and goings. From the standpoint of safety in this place, a guard would be only a useless adornment. Fand was on her own ground here. There were no enemies.

Save one.

Winters opened the door without sound. A maid slept on a low couch. She did not stir as he passed. Beyond an open arch hung with heavy curtains he found the lady Fand.

She slept in a huge carved bed, the bed of the Kings of Valkis. She looked like a child lost in its hugeness. She was very beautiful. Very wicked, and most damnably beautiful.

Winters struck her, quite ruthlessly. Sleep became unconsciousness. There was no outcry. With silks and girdles he found in the room he bound and gagged her, and flung her light weight over his shoulder. Then he went back the way he had come, silently out of the palace.

It was as easy as that. He had not thought it would be

38

easy, but it was. After all, he thought, men seldom guard against the impossible.

Phobos had gone on its careening flight around Mars, and Deimos was too low to give much light. Now carrying the unconscious Fand, now dragging her across the open spaces, Winters made his way back to the amphitheater. In and across the tiered seats to the wall. It was a twenty-foot drop, but he made it as easy as he could on her. He didn't want her dead. Then he slid over, himself, hung briefly by his fingertips, and fell into cushioning brush.

When he got his breath back he made sure that Fand was not hurt. Then he carried her swiftly into the shelter of the unholy garden. Remembering a particularly dense patch of shrubbery near the central clearing, he made for it and crept thankfully into concealment with the heir of all the Kings of Valkis.

Then he waited.

Her eyes were looking up at him in the dim light, bitter gold above the gag of scarlet silk.

"Yes," he said, "you're here, in the garden of Shanga. I brought you here. We have a bargain to talk about, Fand."

He undid the gag, keeping his hand close over her mouth lest she should cry out.

She said, "There will be no bargain between us, Earthman."

"Your life, Fand. Your life for mine, and Jill's and the others here who can still be saved. Destroy the prisms, stop this madness, and you can live to be as old and crazy as your mother."

There was no fear in her. Unbending pride, and hatred, but no fear. She laughed.

He put his hand on her throat, his fingers reaching ironstrong around her neck. "Slim," he said. "Soft, and tender. It would snap so easily."

"Break it, then. Shanga will go on without me. Kor Hal will take over. And you, Burk Winters—you can't escape." Her teeth showed white in a taunting smile. "You'll run with the beasts. No man can break free from Shanga."

Winters nodded. "I know that," he said quietly. "Therefore I must destroy Shanga before it destroys me."

She looked at him, naked and unarmed, crouching in the brush. Once more, she laughed.

He shrugged. "Perhaps it is impossible. I won't know that until it's too late, anyway. It isn't really me I'm worried about, Fand. I could be perfectly happy running on all fours through your garden. Probably I would be perfectly happy hissing and wallowing in the lake. Now the idea sickens me, but after a touch of Shanga it would be all right. No. It isn't me that matters, nor even Jill."

"What, then?"

"Earth has its pride, too," he told her gravely. "It's a younger and cruder pride than yours. It can become pretty ruthless and obnoxious at times, I'll admit. But on the whole, Earth is a good planet, and her people are good people, and she's done more to advance the Solar System than all the other worlds put together. As an Earthman, I don't like to see my world disgraced."

He glanced up and around the amphitheater. "I think," he went on, "that Earth and Mars can learn a lot from each other, if the fanatics on both sides will stop making trouble. You're the worst one I've ever heard of, Fand. You go even beyond fanaticism." He looked at her speculatively. "I think you're as mad right now as your mother."

She did not flare up at that, which convinced him that she was not mad at all, only twisted by the way she lived and the things she had been taught.

She said, "What do you plan to do about all this?"

"Wait. Until dawn, or perhaps later. Anyway, until you've had time to think. Then I shall give you a last chance. After that, I shall kill you."

She was smiling when he replaced the gag, and her eyes did not waver.

The hours passed. Darkness into dawn, and then into full daylight. Winters sat unmoving, his head bowed over his knees. Fand's eyes were closed, and it seemed that she slept.

The garden woke to life with the sun, and all around the dense thicket Winters heard the padding footsteps and the growling of the beasts of Shanga. The things in the shallow lake cried out, and their musky taint soured the wind. Winters shivered like a man with fever and his brooding eyes were haunted.

After a while Jill came. Animal-like she had found him, animal-like she came slipping without sound through the brush. She would have cried out at the sight of Fand, but he silenced her. She crouched beside him, watching him. She was afraid of him and yet she could not stay away. He stroked her shoulder. It was soft and strong and trembling under his hand. Her gaze was doe-like, full of sadness and a bewildered yearning.

Winters' face became as bleak and pitiless as the barren stars that watch from outer space.

The time grew very short. Jill began to look upward toward the prisms. Winters sensed in her a growing nervousness.

He shook Fand. She opened her eyes and looked at him, and he knew what her answer would be before he asked the question.

"Well?"

She shook her head.

For the first time, Winters smiled. "I have decided," he said, "not to kill you, after all."

What he did after that was done quickly and efficiently, and there was no one to see but Jill and Fand. Jill did not understand; the heiress of the Kings of Valkis understood too well.

People began to drift into the amphitheater. Martians, coming to see a show, coming to learn contempt and loathing for the men of Earth. Winters watched them. He was still smiling.

Suddenly he turned to Jill. When he rose a few minutes later, scratched and panting, she was securely bound with strips torn from bonds of Fand. This time she would not bathe so helplessly in the fire of Shanga.

The Martians gathered. Kor Hal came into the royal box, bringing the old woman, who leaned on his arm.

The gong sounded.

V

ONCE AGAIN, Winters watched the gathering of the beasts of Shanga. Hidden in the thicket, beyond the reach of the rays, he saw the hairy bodies rush and jostle toward the

41

central clearing. He saw the shining of their drugged eyes. He heard them moan and whimper, and all over the garden the mouthing whisper went—"*Shanga! Shanga!*"

Jill writhed and thrashed in the agony of her desire, her cries muffled by the wad of silk he had thrust into her mouth. Winters could not bear to look at her. He knew how she was suffering. He was suffering too.

He saw that Kor Hal was leaning forward over the edge of the wall, searching the garden. He knew what the Martian was looking for.

The last notes of the gong rang out. A silence fell on the clearing. Hairy anthropoid, shambling brutes that ran on all fours, nameless creatures beyond the ape, crawling things with wet and shining scales—all silent, all waiting.

The prisms began to glow. The beautiful wicked fire of Shanga filled the air. Burk Winters set his hand between his teeth and bit until the blood ran.

It seemed to him that he could hear a faint thin screaming, rising out of the flowering shrubs by the lake. Low, tough-stemmed shrubs that lay under the full rays of the prisms. *Shanga! Shanga!*

He had to go, into the clearing, into the fiery light. He could not stand it. He must feel again the burning touch on his flesh, the madness and the joy. He could not stay away.

In desperation he flung himself down beside Jill and clung to her, shuddering in torment.

He heard Kor Hal's voice, calling his name.

He steadied himself and rose, stepping out into the full sight of the royal box. The Martians ranged on either side watched him with interest, turning their attention momentarily from the orgy of the beasts of Shanga.

Winters said, "I'm here, Kor Hal."

The man of Barrakesh looked at him and laughed. "Why fight it, Winters? You can't keep away from Shanga."

Winters asked, "Where is your high priestess? Has she wearied of the sport?"

Kor Hal shrugged. "Who knows the mind of the Lady Fand? She comes and goes as she will." He leaned forward. "Go on, Winters! The fire of Shanga is waiting. Look how he sweats there, trying to be a man! Go on, apeling—join your brothers!"

The shrill jeering laughter of the Martians fell upon Winters with the sharpness of spears.

He stood there, naked in the sunlight, his head held stubbornly erect, and he did not move. He could not control the trembling of his limbs nor the harshness of his breathing. The sweat ran in his eyes and blinded him, and the fire of Shanga danced on the writhing bodies, and he thought he would go mad with torment, but he stood there and would not move. He thought he was going to die, but he would not move.

And the Martians watched.

Kor Hal said, "Tomorrow, then. Perhaps the next day—but you'll go, Earthman."

Winters knew that he would. He could not go through this again. If he were still alive in the garden of Shanga the next time the gong sounded, he would go with his brothers.

The fire of Shanga died at last from the prisms, and the creatures of its making lay still on the ground. The Martians sighed. The first stir of departure ran through them.

Burk Winters cried out, "Wait!"

His voice rang back from the empty upper tiers, and it brought every eye upon him. There was desperation in it, and triumph, and the anger of a man driven beyond the bounds of reason.

"Wait, you men of Mars! You came to see a show. Very well, I'll give you one. You, Kor Hal! You told me something, down there in Valkis. You told me of the men of Caer Dhu who first made Shanga, and how in one generation they were destroyed by it. *One* generation."

He stepped forward, finding release for his tortured nerves in this denunciation.

"We of Earth are a young race. We're still close to our beginnings, and for that you hate and mock us, calling us apes. Very well. But that youth gives us strength. We go very slowly down the road of Shanga.

"But you of Mars are old. You have followed the circle of time a long way around, and the end is always close to the beginning. In one generation the men of Caer Dhu were gone. Our fibers are iron, but theirs were only straw.

"That's why no Martian will practice Shanga—why it was forbidden by the City-States. You don't dare to practice it, because it hurls you headlong down that road—toward your end or your beginning, who knows? But you haven't the strength to take it, and you're afraid."

A jeering, angry howl rose from the crowd.

Kor Hal shouted, "Listen to the ape. Listen to the beast we drove through the streets of Valkis!"

"Yes, listen to him!" Winters cried. "Because the Lady Fand is gone, and only the ape knows where she is!"

That silenced them, and in the quiet Winters laughed.

"Perhaps you don't believe me. Shall I tell you how I did it?" He told them, and when he was through telling he listened, while they called him liar, and he jeered in Kor Hal's face.

"Wait," he shouted. "Wait, and I'll bring her to you."

He turned and went toward the clearing. He went fast, because the beasts were already beginning to stir and rouse from their temporary stupor. He remembered from his own experience with Shanga that before consciousness returned there was a period of delirium, so that even in the Trade City solariums the people were not turned loose until it had passed.

Threading his way between the brutish bodies, leaping over them, avoiding the touch of the scaly things, he came to the clump of flowering shrubs by the lake and crawled in among them.

He had not known. He had guessed from Kor Hal's statement that the metamorphosis was swift, but he had not known. There were some things that a man could not even guess at.

In spite of himself, he cried out. He did not want to look at the thing that lay there, did not even want to know that such a form of life had existed, or could exist. But he had to look at it. He had to go close to it, so that he might undo the silken bonds that held it to the roots of the shrubs. He had to touch it. He had to lay his hands upon its softness, lift its flaccid weight, hold its slippery squirming against his own body.

44

It had eyes. That was the worst of it. It had eyes, and it looked at him.

He went away from the thicket, carrying his burden. Back across the clearing, where two great males were already fighting over a she, out into the open space before the royal box, where all could plainly see.

He lifted the thing over his head, high into the sunlight. "Here!" he shouted. "Don't you recognize her? Last of the royal house of Valkis—the Lady Fand!"

Around a portion of the wriggling anatomy that might once have been a neck, the collar of golden plaques swung, shining.

For a moment he held her so, while the faces of the Martians stared like the masks of dead men and Kor Hal rose and gripped the edges of the stone. Then he laid his burden down and stepped back from it where it moved horribly across the turf.

"Look there, you Martians," he said. "That is your own beginning."

In the utter, stricken silence the old woman rose. She stood for a moment, looking down, and it seemed that she was about to speak or cry out, but no sound came. Then she fell, out over the wall and down the sheer drop into the arena. She did not move again.

As though she had led them, the Martians rose with one low terrible cry and followed her. Not to death, as they dropped over the wall, but to vengeance.

Winters ran. He had Jill free in a minute, dragging her away into denser cover. The mouth of the tunnel was not far distant.

The Martians swarmed in upon the clearing, and then the beasts of Shanga saw them. With roars and screams, they surged out to meet their attackers.

Knife and short sword and spiked brass knuckles against fang and claw and the powerful muscles of the brute. The scaly creatures darted here and there, hissing, slashing with their rows of needle-sharp reptilian teeth. Great hands ripped and tore, snapping bones like matchsticks, cracking skulls. And the slim blades flickered in the sunlight, bright tongues speaking death.

Vengeance was done that day in the garden of Shanga.

The vengeance of Earth on Mars, and the vengeance of men upon the shame of their heritage.

Winters saw Kor Hal run his sword through the creeping horror that had been Fand, through and through again until all motion stopped. Then he shouted Winters' name.

Winters went to him.

Neither spoke. There was nothing more to say. Bare-handed, Winters went against the Martian's sword. With the nightmare carnage of the battle going on around them, they two were alone. They two had a special score to settle.

Winters took one long gash above the heart before he caught Kor Hal's arm and broke it. The Martian never whimpered. With his left hand he reached for the knife at his girdle, but it never left the sheath. Winters laid Kor Hal backward across his knee and placed one thigh across his loins and an elbow across his throat. After a moment he dropped the broken body and went away, taking the sword.

The guards came running into the arena through the tunnel.

The fight was spreading outward from the lake. Locked in struggling, swaying knots, the beasts of Shanga slew the Martians and were slain. The waters of the lake were stained red, and the corpse of a Martian was being dragged stealthily into it from the mud of the bank. There was something hidden below the surface, something that could no longer fight on land, but only lay quietly in wait, and fed.

Now the guards had come with their long spears, and Winters knew that in the end there would not be one creature left alive in the garden. And it was well.

He took Jill's hand and led her toward the tunnel, running in the shelter of the trees. The fight was occupying everyone's attention. The brute males were hard to kill, and they fought for the love of it. The tunnel was empty, the gate open, the guards inside the arena, hard at work. Winters and the girl fled through it, taking cover outside the amphitheater just before another group of guards came down from the palace.

From there, with infinite haste and caution, they made their way down the cliffs through the dead ruins of Valkis, and then out across the desert, skirting the living town by the canal. Kor Hal's flier was on the field where Winters remembered it.

He thrust Jill inside, and as he followed her he saw the angry mob start to pour out of Valkis, where word of his crime and his escape had been brought, a little too late.

He took the flier up, setting a course for Kahora. And now that it was all over, he felt a great weariness and an overwhelming desire to forget the very name of Shangra.

But he knew that he could never forget. The golden fire had burned too deep. He knew that he would always be haunted by the beautiful face of Fand as it had looked when he shackled her in the clearing, and by the memory of the high thin screaming as the light poured down from the prisms. Even the psychos could never make him forget.

The governments of Earth and Mars would see to it now that Shanga was stamped out forever. He was glad, and a little proud, because it had been his doing. But even so . . .

He looked over at Jill. Someday, he prayed, she would be herself again. The taint of Shanga would pass her, and she would once more be the Jill Leland he had given his heart to.

But will it pass entirely? For a moment it seemed that he heard the mocking voice of Fand, speaking in his soul. *Will it pass from you, Burk Winters? Can one who has run with the beasts of Shanga ever be the same again?*

He did not know. Looking back, he saw the smoke rising from the unholy garden—and he did not know.

2016: MARS MINUS BISHA

IT WAS close on midnight. Both moons were out of the sky, and there was only blackness below and the mighty blaze of stars above, and between them the old wind dragging its feet in the dust. The Quonset stood by itself, a half mile or so from the canal bank and the town that was on it. Fraser looked at it, thinking what an alien intrusion both it and he were in this place, and wondering if he could stick out the four and a half months still required of him.

The town slept. There was no help for him there. An official order had been given, and so he was tolerated. But he was not welcome. Except in the big trading cities, Earthmen were unwelcome almost anywhere on Mars. It was a lonesome deal.

Fraser began to walk again. He walked a lot at night. The days were ugly and depressing and he spent them inside, working. But the nights were glorious. Not even the driest desert of Earth could produce a sky like this, where the thin air hardly dimmed the luster of the stars. It was the one thing he would miss when he went home.

He walked, dressed warmly against the bitter chill. He brooded, and he watched the stars. He thought about his diminishing whiskey supply and the one hundred and forty-six centuries of written history gone into the dust that blew and tortured his sinuses, and after a while he saw the shadow, the dark shape that moved against the wind, silent, purposeful, and swift.

Out of the northern desert someone was riding.

For the space of three heartbeats Fraser stood rigid and frozen, squinting through the darkness and the starshine at that moving shape. Then he turned and ran for the Quonset. He was not allowed to possess a weapon, and if some of the fanatic northern tribesmen had decided to come and cleanse their desert of his defiling presence, there was little he could do but bar the door and pray.

He did not go inside, just yet. It was unwise to show fear until you had to. He stood by the open door, outside the stream of light that poured from it. He waited, tensed for that final leap.

There was only a single rider, mounted on one of the big scaly beasts the Martian nomads use as the Earthly desertfolk use camels. Fraser relaxed a little, but not too much. One man with a spear could be enough. The stranger came slowly into the light, wrapped and muffled against the night, curbing with a strong hand the uneasy hissings and shyings of the beast at the unfamiliar smells that came to it from the Quonset. Fraser leaned forward, and suddenly the weakness of relief came over him. The rider was a woman, and she carried before her on the saddle pad a child, almost hidden in the folds of her cloak.

Fraser gave her the courteous Martian greeting. She looked down at him, tall and fierce-eyed, hating and yet somehow desperate, and presently she said, "You are the Earthman, the doctor."

"Yes."

The child slept, its head lolled back against the woman's body. There was something unnatural in the way it slept, undisturbed by the light or the voices. Fraser said gently, "I am here only to help."

The woman's arm tightened around the child. She looked at Fraser, and then in through the open door at the unfamiliar alien things that were there. Her face, made grim and hard by hunger and long marches, and far too proud for weeping, crumpled suddenly toward tears. She lifted the bridle chain and swung the beast around, but before he had gone his own length she curbed him again. When she had turned once more toward Fraser she was calm as stone.

"My child is—ill," she said, very quietly, hesitating over that one word.

Fraser held up his arms. "I'll see what I can do."

The child—a girl. Fraser saw now, perhaps seven years old—did not stir even when she was lifted down from the saddle pad. Fraser started to carry her inside, saying over his shoulder to the woman, "I'll need to ask some questions. You can watch while I examine—"

A wild harsh cry and a thunder of padded hooves drowned out his words. He whirled around, and then he ran a little way, shouting, with the child in his arms, but it was no use. The woman was bent low in the saddle, urging the beast on with that frantic cry, digging in the spurs, and in a minute she was gone, back into the desert and the night. Fraser stood staring after her, openmouthed, and swearing, and looking helplessly at the girl. There was an ominous finality about the way the woman had left. Why? Even if the child was dying, wouldn't a mother wait to know? Even if the sickness was contagious, would she ride the Lord knew how many miles across the desert with her, and then run?

There were no answers to those questions. Fraser gave up and went into the Quonset, kicking the door shut behind him. Passing through his combination living quarters and office, he went into the tiny infirmary which adjoined his equally small but well-equipped lab. Neither office nor infirmary had had many customers. The Martians preferred their own methods, their own healers. Fraser was not supposed, anyway, to be the local G.P. The Medical Foundation grant and the order of the Martian authorities permitting him to be here both stated that he was engaged in research on certain viruses. Noncooperation of the populace had not made his work any easier.

He became suddenly hopeful about the child.

Some two hours later he put her, still sleeping, into the neat white bed and sat down in the room outside, where he could watch her through the open door. He had a drink, and then another, and lighted a cigarette with hands that had trouble putting flame and tip together.

She was sound as a dollar. Thin, a bit undersized and undernourished like most Martian youngsters, but healthy. There was nothing whatever the matter with her, except that someone had thoroughly drugged her.

Fraser rose and flung open the outer door. He went out, staring with a kind of desperation into the north, straining his ears for a sound of hooves. Dawn was not far off. The wind was rising, thickening the lower air with dust, dimming the stars. Out on the desert nothing moved, nor was there any sound.

For the rest of that night and most of the morning that came after it, Fraser sat unmoving by the child's bed, waiting for her to wake.

She did it quietly. One moment her face was as it had been, remote and secret, and in the next she had opened her eyes. Her small body stirred and stretched, she yawned, and then she looked at Fraser, very solemnly but without surprise. He smiled and said, "Hello."

She sat up, a dark and shaggy-haired young person, with eyes the color of topaz, and the customary look of premature age and wisdom that the children of Mars share with the children of the Earthly East. She asked hesitantly, "My mother—?"

"She had to go away for a while," Fraser said, and added with false assurance, "but she'll be back soon." He was comforting himself as much as the child.

She took even that shred of hope from him. "No," she said. "She will not come back." She laid her head between her knees and began to cry, not making any fuss about it. Fraser put his arm around her.

"Here," he said. "Here now, don't do that. Of course she'll come back for you; she's your mother."

"She can't."

"But why? Why did she bring you here? You're not sick; you don't need a doctor."

The child said simply, "They were going to kill me."

Fraser was silent for a long time. Then he said, "What?"

The thin shoulders quivered under his arm. "They said I made the sickness that was in our tribe. The Old Men came, all together, and they told my father and mother I had to be killed. The Old Men are very powerful in magic, but they said they could not make me clean." She broke off, choking over a sob. "My mother said it was her right to do the thing, and she took me way off into the desert. She cried. She never did that before. I was frightened, and then she told me she wasn't going to hurt me, she was going to take me where I would be safe. She gave me some

52

bitter water to drink, and told me not to be afraid. She talked to me until I went to sleep."

She looked up at Fraser, a frightened and bewildered little girl, and yet with a dignity about her, too.

"My mother said our gods have cursed me, and I would never be safe with my own people any more. But she said Earthmen have different gods, who wouldn't know me. She said you wouldn't kill me. Is that true?"

Fraser said something under his breath, and then he told her, "Yes. That's true. Your mother is a wise woman. She brought you to the right place." His face had become perfectly white. He stepped back from the bed and asked, "What's your name?"

"Bisha."

"Are you hungry, Bisha?"

She hesitated, still gulping down sobs. "I don't know."

"You think about it. Your clothes are there—put them on. I'll fix some breakfast."

He went out into the next room, sick and shaking with rage such as he had never experienced before. Superstition, ignorance, the pious cruelty of the savage. Get an epidemic going and when the magic of the Old Man fails, find a scapegoat. Call a child accursed, and send its own mother to slaughter it. Mentally, Fraser bowed to the fierce-eyed woman who had been too tough for those cowardly old men. Poor devil, only the certainty of death could have made her abandon her child to an Earthman—a creature alien and unknown, but having different gods—

"Why would they curse me?" asked Bisha, close behind him. "Our gods, I mean." Dressing was an easy proposition for her, with one thick garment to pull over her head, and sandals for her feet. Her hair hung over her face and the tears still dripped, and now her nose was running, and Fraser didn't know whether to laugh or cry. "They didn't," he said, and picked her up. "It's only superstitious nonsense—"

He stopped. That was not going to do. Seven years, a lifetime of training and belief, were not going to be wiped out by a few words from a stranger. He stood scowling, trying hard to think of a way to reach her, and then he became aware that she was looking at him with a child's

53

intense and wondering stare, sitting quite stiffly in his arms. He asked, "Are you afraid of me?"

"I—I've never seen anyone like you before."

"Hm. And you've never seen a house like this one, either?"

She glanced around, and shook her head. "No. It's—" She had no words for what it was, only a shiver of awe.

Fraser smiled. "Bisha, you told me the Old Men of your tribe were very powerful in magic."

"Oh, yes!"

He set her down and took her hand firmly in his. "I'm going to show you a few things. Come on."

He didn't know whether child psychologists and other ethical persons would approve of his method, but it was the only one he could think of. With the imposing air of one performing wonders, he introduced the child of the nomad tents to the miracles of modern gadgetry, from running water to record music and micro-books. As a climax, he permitted her to peer in through the door of the laboratory, at the mystic and glittering tangle of glass and chrome. And he asked her, "Are your Old Men greater in magic than I?"

"No." She had drawn away from him, her hands clutched tightly around her as though to avoid the accident of touching anything. Behind her from the living quarters Wagner's *Fire Music* still roared and rippled, out of a tiny spool of wire. Suddenly Bisha was down on her knees in an attitude of complete submission. "You are the greatest doctor in the world."

Her word for "doctor" meant the same as "shaman." Fraser felt contrite and ashamed. It seemed a shabby trick to impress a child. But he stuck to it, saying solemnly, "Very well, Bisha. And now that that is understood, I tell you that curses have no power in this place, and I want no more talk of them."

She listened, not raising her head.

"You are safe here. You are not to be afraid. Look up at me, Bisha. Do you promise not to be afraid?"

She looked up. He smiled, and after a little she smiled back. "I promise."

"Good," he said, and held out his hand. "Let's eat."

About then it dawned on Fraser that he was saddled with a child. For the four and a half months that remained of his term here he would have to feed, look after her and keep her hidden. The people of the town would hardly shelter her—Bisha's mother hadn't trusted them, certainly—and if they did, the nomads would only find her again when they came in for the fall trading. The only other alternative was the central government at Karappa, which would surely not condone ritual murder, but that was three hundred miles away. He had a trac-car, but the work going forward in the lab would not wait for him to trundle a slow six hundred miles up and down the desert. He could not possibly leave it.

Four and a half months. He looked down at the small figure pattering beside him, and wondered what in the devil he was going to do with her all that time.

At the end of a week he would have been lost without her. The awful loneliness and isolation of the Quonset was gone. There was another voice in the place, another presence, somebody to sit across the table from him, somebody to talk to. Bisha was no trouble. She had been brought up not to be a trouble, in a hard school where survival was the supreme lesson, and that same school had impressed on her young mind the wisdom of making the best of things. She was no trouble at all. She was company, the first he had had in nearly nine months. He liked her.

Mostly she was cheerful and alert, too much engrossed in a new world of marvels to brood about the past. But she had her moods. Fraser found her one afternoon huddled in a corner, dull and spiritless, in the depths of a depression that seemed almost too deep for tears. He thought he knew what the trouble was. He took her on his lap and said, "Are you lonesome, Bisha?"

She whispered, "Yes."

He tried to talk to her. It was like talking to a blank wall. At last he said helplessly, "Try not to miss them too much, Bisha. I know I'm not the same as your own family, and this place is strange to you, but try."

"You're good," she murmured. "I like you. It isn't that. I was lonesome before, sometimes."

"Lonesome for what, Bisha?"

"I don't know. Just—lonesome."

Queer little tyke, thought Fraser, *but then most kids are queer to adult eyes, full of emotions so new and untried that they don't know quite how to come out. And no wonder she's depressed. In her spot, who wouldn't be?*

He put her to bed early, and then, feeling unusually tired after a long day's work, he turned in himself.

He was awakened by Bisha, shaking him, sobbing, calling his name. Leaden and half dazed, he started up in alarm, asking her what was the matter, and she whimpered, "I was afraid. You didn't wake up."

"What do you mean, I didn't wake up?" He sank back again, weighted down with the sleep he had not finished, and began to bawl her out. Then he happened to look at the clock.

He had slept a trifle over fourteen hours.

Mechanically he patted Bisha and begged her pardon. He tried to think, and his brain was wrapped in layers of cotton wool, dull, lethargic. He had had one drink before going to bed, not enough to put anyone out for one hour, let alone fourteen. He had not done anything physically exhausting. He had been tired, but nothing the usual eight hours wouldn't cure. Something was wrong, and a small pinpoint of fear began to prick him.

He asked, "How long have you been trying to wake me?"

She pointed to a chair that stood beside the window. "When I began, its shadow was there. Now it is there."

As near as he could figure, about two hours. Not sleep, then. Semi-coma. The pinprick became a knife blade.

Bisha said, so low that he could hardly hear her, "It is the sickness that was in our tribe. I have brought it to you."

"You might have at that," Fraser muttered. He had begun to shiver, from the onset of simple panic. He was so far away from help. It would be so easy to die here, walled in by the endless miles of desert.

The child had withdrawn herself from him. "You see," she said, "the curse has followed me."

With an effort, Fraser got hold of himself. "It hasn't anything to do with curses. There are people we call carriers—

Listen, Bisha, you've got to help me. This sickness—did any of your tribesmen die of it?"

"No—"

Frasher trembled even more violently, this time from sheer relief. "Well, then, it's not so bad, is it? How does it—"

"The Old Men said they *would* die unless I was taken away and killed." She had retreated even farther now, to the other side of the room, to the door. Suddenly she turned and ran.

It was a minute before Fraser's numbed brain understood. Then he staggered up and followed her, out into the dust and the cold light, shouting her name. He saw her, a tiny figure running between the blue-black sky and the dull red desolation, and he ran too, fighting the weakness and the lassitude that were on him. He seemed to run for hours with the chill wind and the dust, and then he overtook her. She struggled, begging to be let go, and he smacked her. After that she was quiet. He picked her up, and she wailed, "I don't want you to die!"

Fraser looked out across the pitiless desert and held her tight. "Do you love me that much, Bisha?"

"I have eaten your bread, and your roof has sheltered me—" The old ceremonial phrases learned from her elders sounded odd in her young mouth, but perfectly sincere. "You are my family now, my mother and my father. I don't want my curse to fall on you."

For a moment Fraser found it hard to speak. Then he said gently, "Bisha, is your wisdom greater than mine?"

She shook her head.

"Is it your right to question it?"

"No."

"What is your right, Bisha, as a child?"

"To obey."

"You are never to do this again. Never, no matter what happens, are you to run away from me. Do you hear me, Bisha?"

She looked up at him. "You're not afraid of the curse, even now?"

"Not now, or any other time."

"You *want* me to stay?"

"Of course I do, you poor wretched little idiot!"

She smiled, gravely, with the queer dignity he had seen in her before. "You are a very great doctor," she said. "You will find a way to lift the curse. I'm not afraid, now."

She lay warm and light in the circle of his arms, and he carried her back to the Quonset, walking slowly, talking all the way. It was odd talk, in that time and place. It was about a far-off city called San Francisco, and a white house on a cliff that looked out over a great bay of blue water. It was about trees and birds and fishes and green hills, and all the things a little girl could do among them and be happy. In the past few minutes Fraser had forgotten Karappa and the authorities of Mars. In the past few minutes he had acquired a family.

Back in the lab Fraser began work. He questioned Bisha about the sickness as she had seen it in her tribe. Apparently the seizures came at irregular intervals and involved nothing more than the comatose sleep, but he gathered that the periods of unconsciousness had been much shorter, often no more than a few minutes. That could be accounted for by acquired resistance on the part of the Martians. Bisha, of course, had never had the sickness, and Fraser imagined that the accident of natural immunity had caused her to be picked for the tribal scapegoat.

His own symptoms were puzzling. No temperature, no pain, no physical derangement, only the lassitude and weakness, and by next morning they had passed off. He consulted his books on Martian pathology. There was nothing in them. He ran a series of exhaustive tests, even to a spinal tap on Bisha, which she took to be a very potent ritual of exorcism. He would rather have done one on himself, but that was impossible, and there might be evidence in the child of some latent organism.

The test was negative. All the tests were negative. He and Bisha were as healthy as horses.

Baffled but intensely relieved, Fraser began to think of other explanations for the ailment. It was not a disease, so it must be a side-effect of some physical condition, perhaps the light gravitation or pressure, or the thin atmosphere, or all three, that affected Martians as well as Earthmen, but in a lesser degree. He made a detailed report, thrusting into the back of his mind as a small worry that no such side-effect had ever been observed before.

He waited nervously for a recurrence. It didn't come, and as the work in the lab demanded more and more of his attention he began to forget about it. The time that he woke up in his chair with an untasted drink beside him and no memory of having gone to sleep he put down resolutely to weariness and overwork. Bisha had retired with another fit of the blues, so she knew nothing about that, and he didn't mention it. She seemed to be getting over the curse fixation, and he wanted to keep it that way.

More time went by. Bisha was learning English, and she could name all the trees that stood around that house in San Francisco. The confinement in the small hut was getting them both down, and she was as anxious to leave as Fraser, but apart from that everything was going well.

And then the nomads came in from the desert for the fall trading.

Fraser barred the doors and drew the blinds. For three days and nights of the trading he and Bisha hid inside, with the distant sound of the pipes and the shouting coming to them muffled but poignant, the music and the voices of Bisha's own people, her own family among the tribes. They were hard days. At the end of them Bisha retired again into the remoteness of her private grief, and Fraser let her alone. On the fourth morning the nomads were gone.

Fraser thanked whatever gods there were. Weary and dragged out, he went into the lab, hating the work now because it took so much out of him, anxious to have it finished. He started across the room to open the blind—

He was lying on the floor. The lights were on and it was night. Bisha was beside him. She seemed to have been there a long time. His arm ached. There were clumsy wrappings on it, stained with blood. Shards of glass littered the end of the lab bench and the floor. The familiar leaden numbness pervaded his whole body. It was hard to move, hard to think. Bisha crept to him and laid her head on his chest, silently, like a dog.

Very slowly Fraser's head cleared, and thoughts came into it. *I must have fallen across the bench. Good God, what if I had broken the virus cultures? Not only us, the whole*

town— I might have bled to death, and what would happen
to Bisha? Suppose I did die, what would happen to her?

It took longer this time to return to normal. He stitched
up the cuts in his arm, and the job was not neat. He was
afraid. He was afraid to leave his chair, afraid to smoke,
afraid to operate the stove. The hours crawled by, the rest
of the night, another day, another evening. He felt better,
but fear had grown into desperation. He had only Bisha's
word that this illness was not fatal. He began to distrust
his own tests, postulating alien organisms unrecognizable
to the medical science he knew. He was afraid for himself.
He was terrified for Bisha.

He said abruptly, "I am going into the town."

"Then I will come with you."

"No. You'll stay right here. I'll be all right. There is a
doctor in the town, a Martian healer. He may know—"

He went out, into the bitter darkness and the blazing of
the stars. It seemed a long way to the town.

He passed the irrigated land, stripped of its harvest, and
came into the narrow streets. The town was not old as they
go on Mars, but the mud brick of the walls had been patched
and patched again, fighting a losing battle with the dry wind
and the scouring dust. There were few people abroad. They
looked at Fraser and passed him by, swarthy folk, hot-eyed
and perpetually desperate. The canal was their god, their
mother and their father, their child and their wife. Out of
its dark channel they drew life, painfully, drop by drop. They
did not remember who had cut it, all the long miles from
the polar cap across the dead sea bottoms, across the deserts
and through the tunnels underneath the hills. They only
knew that it was there, and that it was better for a man
to sin the foulest sin than to neglect the duty that was on
him to keep the channel clear. A cruel life, and yet they
lived it, and were content.

There were no torches to light the streets, but Fraser
knew the house he wanted. The door of corroded metal
opened reluctantly to his knock and closed swiftly behind
him. The room was small, lit by a smoky lamp and barely
warmed by a fire of roots, but on the walls there were
tapestries of incalculable age and incredible value.

Tor-Esh, the man of healing, did well at his trade. His

robe was threadbare, but his belly protruded and his chops were plump, unusual things among his lean people. He was fetish-priest, oracle,. and physician, and he was the only man of the town who had shown any interest in Fraser and his work. It was not necessarily a friendly interest.

He gave Fraser the traditional greeting, and Fraser said stiffly, "I need your help. I have contracted an illness—"

Tor-Esh listened. His eyes were shrewd and penetrating, and the smile that was habitually on his face left them untouched. As Fraser talked, even that pretense of a smile went gradually away.

When he was finished, Tor-Esh said, "Again. More slowly, please, your Martian is not always clear."

"But do you know what it is? Can you tell me—"

Tor-Esh said, "Again!"

Fraser repeated the things he had said, trying not to show the fear that was in him. Tor-Esh asked questions. Accurate questions. Fraser answered them. For a little bit Tor-Esh was silent, heavy-faced and grim in the flickering light, and Fraser waited with his heart pounding in his throat.

Tor-Esh said slowly, "You are not ill. But unless a certain thing is done, you will surely die."

Fraser spoke in anger. "Talk sense! A healthy man doesn't fall off his feet. A healthy man doesn't die, except by accident."

"In some ways," said Tor-Esh very softly, "we are an ignorant people. It is not because we have not learned. It is because we have forgotten."

"I'm sorry, I didn't mean— Look, I came to you for help. This is something I don't understand, something I can't cope with."

"Yes." Tor-Esh moved to the window, dark in the thickness of the wall. "Have you thought of the canal? Not only this one, but the many canals that bind Mars in a great net. Have you thought how they must have been built? The machines, the tremendous power that would have been needed, to make a dying world live yet a little longer. We are the children of the men who conceived and built them, and yet nothing is left to us but the end product of their work, and we must grub with our hands in the channel, digging out the blown sand."

"I know," said Fraser impatiently. "I've studied Martian history. But what—"

"Many centuries," said Tor-Esh, as though he had not heard. "Nations and empires, wars and pestilences, and kings beyond the counting. Learning. Science. Growth and splendor, and weariness, and decay. Oceans have rolled away into dust, the mountains have fallen down, and the sources of power are used up. Can you conceive, you who come from a young world, how many races have evolved on Mars?"

He turned to face the Earthman. "You have come with your thundering ships, your machines and your science, giving the lie to our gods, who we thought had created no other men but us. You look upon us as degraded and without knowledge—and yet you too are an ignorant people, not because you have forgotten, but because you have not yet learned. There are many sciences, many kinds of knowledge. There have been races on Mars who could build the canals. There were others who could see without eyes and hear without ears, who could control the elements and cause men to live or die as they willed it, who were so powerful that they were stamped out because men feared them. They are forgotten now, but their blood is in us. And sometimes a child is born—"

Fraser stiffened.

Tor-Esh said quietly, "There was talk among the nomads about a child."

Nerves, drawing tight in Fraser's belly. Fear-nerves, and a chill sweat. *I never mentioned Bisha. How could he know*—

"I'm not interested in folklore. Just tell me—"

"There was a certain evil in the tribe. When the child was taken away, the evil departed. Now it is in your house. It seems that the mother lied. The child is not dead. She is with you."

"Witchcraft and sorcery," Fraser snarled. "Curses and cowardice. I thought you knew better, Tor-Esh." He started for the door. "I was a fool to come here."

Tor-Esh moved swiftly and placed his hand on the latch, that it might not be lifted until he was through.

"We are ignorant folk, but still we do not kill children because we find pleasure in it. As for witchcraft and sorcery —words are words. Only facts have meaning. If you wish to die, that is your affair. But when you are dead the child must come into the town—and that is our affair. I will send word to the nomads. The girl is theirs, and the duty belongs to them; we do not wish it. But until they come I will set a wall around your house. You are likely to die quite soon. There were twenty in her tribe to share the curse, but you are alone, and we can take no chances."

Seeing, perhaps, the absolute horror in Fraser's face, Tor-Esh added, "It will be done mercifully. We bear the child no hate."

He lifted the latch, and Fraser went into the narrow street. He turned toward the desert, and when he had crossed the plowed land he began to run. He ran fast, but a rider passed him, speeding into the desert on the track of the caravan.

Bisha was waiting for him, sleepily anxious. He said, "You know where the food is. Pack as much as you can in the trac-car. Blankets, too. Hurry up, we're leaving."

He went into the laboratory. In violent haste, but with the utmost care, he destroyed the work of months, tempted as he did so to forget ethics and scatter his virus cultures broadcast into the town. Evil. Superstition. Legendary warlocks, tales of mighty wizards. He had read some of the old imaginative stories, written before space flight, in which ruthless Earthmen were pictured trampling innocent Mars under their feet. Logic and logistics both had made that impossible, when it came to the unromantic reality, and he was almost sorry. He would have liked to trample some Martians under his feet.

When the laboratory was cleansed, he threw his notes together in a steel box and took them into the dust-tight shed at the back of the Quonset where the trac-car was housed. Bisha, tear-streaked and silent, had been patiently lugging supplies. He checked them rapidly, added a few more, and swung the child up into the cab. She looked at him, and he realized then that she was frightened. "Don't worry," he told her. "We're going to be all right."

"You're not taking me back?"

He said savagely, "I'm taking you to the Terran consulate at Karappa, and after that I'm taking you to San Francisco. And nobody had better try to stop me."

He flung open the shed door and climbed in beside her. The trac-car rolled out clanking across the sand. And already there were lines of torches, streaming out from the town, flung across his way.

He said, "Crouch down on the floor, Bisha, and stay there. You won't get hurt."

He poured on the power. The trac-car lurched forward, snorting and raising a great cloud of dust. He headed it straight for the wavering line of torches, ducking his head instinctively so that he was pressed close to the wheel. The cab was metal, and the glass parts of it were theoretically unbreakable, but he could see now in the torchlight the bright metal throwing-sticks of the townsmen, the swift boomerangs that could take off a man's head as neatly as a knife blade. He ducked.

Something hit the window beside him, starring it with a million cracks. Other things whacked and rattled viciously against the car. The torches fell away from in front of him, taking with them the dark startled faces of the men who held them. He was through the line. The open desert was before him. Three hundred miles, Karappa, and civilization.

If he could beat the nomads.

He had better beat them. It was his neck as well as Bisha's. He needed care. He needed it fast, from somebody who did not believe in curses.

Dawn came, cold in a dark sky, veiled in dust. There was no canal between them and Karappa, no town, nothing but the fine dry sand that flowed like water under the wind.

"Look here," he said to Bisha. "If I should suddenly fall asleep—" He showed her how to stop the trac-car. "At once, Bisha. And stay inside the cab until I wake again." She nodded, her lips pressed tight with the effort of concentration. He made her do it several times until he was sure she would not forget.

The miles flowed out before and behind, to left and to right, featureless, unbroken. How long would it take a single rider to catch a laden caravan? How long for the desert men on their fleet beasts to find a trail? The sand was soft and the clanking treads sank in it, and no matter how much you wanted to hurry you could go no faster than the desert would let you.

Bisha had been thinking hard. Suddenly she said, "They will follow us."

She was smart, too smart for her own good. Fraser said, "The nomads? We can beat them. Anyway, they'll soon give up."

"No, they'll follow. Not you, but me. And they will kill us both."

Fraser said, "We're going to Earth. The men of Mars, and the gods of Mars, can't reach there."

"They are very powerful gods— Are you sure?"

"Very sure. You'll be happy on Earth, Bisha."

She sat close to him, and after a while she slept. There was a compass on the dash, a necessity in that place of no roads and no landmarks. Fraser kept the needle centered, setting a course as though with a ship. Time and the sand rolled on, and he was tired.

Tired.

You are likely to die quite soon—there were twenty in her tribe to share the curse—

The desert whispered. The sounds of the trac-car were accepted and forgotten by the ear, and beyond them the desert whispered, gliding, sliding, rippling under the wind. Fraser's vision blurred and wavered. He should not have pushed himself so hard at the work. Tired, no resistance to the sickness. That was why it had been light among the hardy nomads, more serious in him, an alien already worn down by months of confinement and mental strain. That was why.

—twenty in her tribe to share it—but you, alone—

Three hundred miles isn't so far. Of course you can make it. You've made it in an afternoon, on Earth.

This isn't Earth. And you didn't make it in a cold creeping desert.

You, alone—

Damn Tor-Esh!

"Bisha, wake up. We need some food. And first off, I need that bottle."

With a drink and some food inside him he felt better. "We'll keep on all night. By morning, easy, we'll be in Karappa. If the nomads are following, they'll never catch up."

65

Mid-afternoon, and he was driving in a daze. He lost track of the compass. When he noticed it again he was miles off his course. He sat for some minutes trying to remember the correct reading, trembling. Bisha watched him.

"Don't look so frightened," he said. His voice rose. "I'm all right. I'll get us there!"

She hung her head and looked away from him.

"And don't cry, damn it! Do you hear? I've got enough on my neck without you being doleful."

"It is because of me," she said. "You should have believed the words of the Old Men."

He struck her, the first time he had ever laid his hand on her in anger. "I don't want any more of that talk. If you haven't learned better in all this time—"

She retreated to the other side of the seat. He got the trac-car going again, in the right direction, but he did not go far. He had to rest. Just an hour's sleep would help. He stopped. He looked at Bisha, and like something that had happened years ago he remembered that he had slapped her.

"Poor little Bisha," he said, "and it isn't any of it your fault. Will you forgive me?"

She nodded, and he kissed her, and she cried a little, and then he went to sleep, telling her to wake him when the hand on the dashboard clock reached five. It was hard to rouse when the time came, and it was full dark before the trac-car was lurching and bucking its way out of the sand that had drifted around it. Fraser was not refreshed. He felt worse, if anything, sapped and drained, his brain as empty as an upturned bucket.

He drove.

He was off his course again. He must have dozed, and the car had made a circle to the south. He turned angrily to Bisha and said, "Why didn't you stop the car? I told you—"

In the faint glow from the dashboard he saw her face, turned toward the desert, and he knew the look on it, the withdrawal and the sadness. She did not answer. Fraser swore. Of all the times to pick for a fit of the blues, when he needed her so badly! She had enough to make her moody, but it was getting to be a habit, and she had no right to indulge her emotions now. She had already cost them precious hours, precious miles. He reached out and shook her.

It was like shaking a rag doll. He spoke to her sharply. She seemed not to hear. Finally he stopped the car, furious with her stubbornness, and wrenched her around to face him. For the second time he slapped her.

She did not weep. She only whispered, "I can't help it. They used to punish me too, but I can't help it."

She didn't seem to care. He couldn't touch her, couldn't penetrate. He had never tried to shake her out of these moods before. Now he found that he could not. He let her sink back into the corner, and he looked at her, and a slow corrosive terror began to creep through him because of the times before—the times that she had been like this.

The times immediately preceding the periods of blackness, the abnormal sleep.

A pattern. Every time, the same unvaried pattern.

But it made no sense. It was only coincidence.

Coincidence, three times repeated? And how had Tor-Esh known so certainly that the child was with him?

Three times, the pattern. If it happened a fourth time, it could not be coincidence. If it happened a fourth time, he would know.

Could he afford a fourth time?

Crazy. How could a child's moods affect a man?

He grabbed her again. A desperation came over him. He treated her roughly, more roughly than he could ever have dreamed of treating a child. And it did no good. She looked at him with remote eyes and bore it without protest, without interest.

Not a mood, then. Something else.

What?

Sometimes a child is born—

Fraser sent the trac-car rushing forward along the beam from its headlights, a bright gash in the immemorial dark.

He was afraid. He was afraid of Bisha. And still he would not believe.

Get to Karappa. There's help there. Whatever it is there'll be somebody to know the truth, to do something. Keep awake; don't let the curtain fall again.

Think. We know it isn't a curse; that's out. We know it isn't a disease. We know it isn't side-effects; they'd have been observed. Besides, Tor-Esh understood.

What was it he said about old races? What did they teach us about them in the colleges? Too much, and not enough. Too many races, and not enough time.

They could see without eyes and hear without ears, they could control the elements—

He tried to remember, and it was a pain and a torment. He looked at the child. Old races. Recessive genes, still cropping out. But what's the answer? ESP is known among the Martians, but this isn't ESP. What, then?

A remnant, a scrap of something twisted out of shape and incomplete?

What is she so lonesome for, that she doesn't know?

The answer came to him suddenly, clear as the ringing of a bell. A page from a forgotten textbook, horded all these years in his subconscious, a casual mention of a people who had tried to sublimate the conditions of a dying world by establishing a kind of mental symbiosis, living in a tight community, sharing each others' minds and their potentials, and who had succeeded in acquiring by their mass effort such powers of mental control that for several centuries they had ruled this whole quadrant of Mars, leaving behind them a host of legends.

And a child.

A child normal and healthy in every way but one. Her brain was incomplete, designed by a cruel trick of heredity to be one of a community of interdependent minds that no longer existed. Like a battery, it discharged its electrical energy in the normal process of thinking and living, and like a run-down battery it must be charged again from outside, because its own regenerative faculty was lacking. And so it stole from the unsuspecting minds around it, an innocent vampire draining them whenever it felt the need.

It was draining his now. There had been twenty in her tribe, and so none of them had died as yet. But he was alone. And that was why the intervals had shortened, because he could no longer satisfy her need.

And the Martians in their ignorance were right. And he in his wisdom had been wrong.

68

If he put her out now, and left her in the desert, he would be safe.

He stopped the car and looked at her. She was so little and helpless, and he had come to love her. It wasn't her fault. Something might still be done for her, a way might be found, and in a city she would not be so deadly.

Could he survive another plunge into the darkness?

He didn't know. But she had run away once of her own accord, for his sake. He could do no less than try.

He took her into his arms.

The curtain dropped.

Fraser woke slowly, in brazen sunshine and a great silence. As one creeping back from the edge of an abyss he woke, and the car was very still. There was no one in it with him. He called, but there was no answer.

He got out of the car. He walked, calling, and then he saw the tracks. The tracks of the nomads' beasts, coming toward the car from behind. The small tracks of Bisha's feet, going back to meet them.

He stopped calling. The sound of his voice was too loud, too terrible. He began to run, back along that trail. It ended in a little huddle of clothing that had no life in it.

She had broken her promise to him. She had disobeyed and left him, asleep and safe, to meet the riders by herself, the riders who were following her, not him.

So small a grave did not take long to dig.

Fraser drove on. There was no more danger now, but he drove fast, seeing the desert in a blur, wanting only Earth —but not a white house there that for him would be forever haunted.

2024:   THE LAST DAYS OF SHANDAKOR

I

HE CAME ALONE into the wine shop, wrapped in a dark
red cloak, with the cowl drawn over his head. He stood for
a moment by the doorway and one of the slim dark predatory
women who live in those places went to him, with a silvery
chiming from the little bells that were almost all she wore.

I saw her smile up at him. And then, suddenly, the smile
became fixed and something happened to her eyes. She was
no longer looking at the cloaked man but through him. In the
oddest fashion—it was as though he had become invisible.

She went by him. Whether she passed some word along
or not I couldn't tell but an empty space widened around
the stranger. And no one looked at him. They did not avoid
looking at him. They simply refused to see him.

He began to walk slowly across the crowded room. He
was very tall and he moved with a fluid, powerful grace
that was beautiful to watch. People drifted out of his way,
not seeming to, but doing it. The air was thick with nameless smells, shrill with the laughter of women.

Two tall barbarians, far gone in wine, were carrying on
some intertribal feud and the yelling crowd had made room
for them to fight. There was a silver pipe and drum and
a double-banked harp making old wild music. Lithe brown
bodies leaped and whirled through the laughter and the
shouting and the smoke.

The stranger walked through all this, alone, untouched,
unseen. He passed close to where I sat. Perhaps because I,

of all the people in that place, not only saw him but stared at him, he gave me a glance of black eyes from under the shadow of his cowl—eyes like blown coals, bright with suffering and rage.

I caught only a glimpse of his muffled face. The merest glimpse—but that was enough. *Why did he have to show his face to me in that wine shop in Barrakesh?*

He passed on. There was no space in the shadowy corner where he went but space was made, a circle of it, a moat between the stranger and the crowd. He sat down. I saw him lay a coin on the outer edge of the table. Presently a serving wench came up, picked up the coin and set down a cup of wine. But it was as if she waited on an empty table.

I turned to Kardak, my head drover, a Shunni with massive shoulders and uncut hair braided in an intricate tribal knot. "What's all that about?" I asked.

Kardak shrugged. "Who knows?" He started to rise. "Come, JonRoss, it is time we got back to the serai."

"We're not leaving for hours yet. And don't lie to me; I've been on Mars a long time. What is that man? Where does he come from?"

Barrakesh is the gateway between north and south. Long ago, when there were oceans in equatorial and southern Mars, when Valkis and Jekkara were proud seats of empire and not thieves' dens, here on the edge of the northern Drylands the great caravans had come and gone to Barrakesh for a thousand thousand years. It is a place of strangers.

In the time-eaten streets of rock you see tall Keshi hillmen, nomads from the high plains of Upper Shun, lean dark men from the south who barter away the loot of forgotten tombs and temples, cosmopolitan sophisticates up from Kahora and the Trade Cities, where there are spaceports and all the appurtenances of modern civilization.

The red-cloaked stranger was none of these.

A glimpse of a face— I am a planetary anthropologist. I was supposed to be charting Martian ethnology and I was doing it on a fellowship grant I had wangled from a Terran university too ignorant to know that the vastness of Martian history makes such a project hopeless.

I was in Barrakesh, gathering an outfit preparatory to a

year's study of the tribes of Upper Shun. And suddenly there had passed close by me a man with golden skin and un-Martian black eyes and a facial structure that belonged to no race I knew. I have seen the carven faces of fauns that were a little like it.

Kardak said again, "It is time to go, JonRoss!"

I looked at the stranger, drinking his wine in silence and alone. "Very well, I'll ask him."

Kardak sighed. "Earthmen," he said, "are not given much to wisdom." He turned and left me.

I crossed the room and stood beside the stranger. In the old courteous High Martian they speak in all the Low Canal towns I asked permission to sit.

Those raging, suffering eyes met mine. There was hatred in them, and scorn, and shame. "What breed of human are you?"

"I am an Earthman."

He said the name over as though he had heard it before and was trying to remember. "Earthman. Then it is as the winds have said, blowing across the desert—that Mars is dead and men from other worlds defile her dust." He looked out over the wine shop and all the people who would not admit his presence. "Change," he whispered. "Death and change and the passing away of things."

The muscles of his face drew tight. He drank and I could see now that he had been drinking for a long time, for days, perhaps for weeks. There was a quiet madness on him.

"Why do the people shun you?"

"Only a man of Earth would need to ask," he said and made a sound of laughter, very dry and bitter.

I was thinking, a *new race, an unknown race!* I was thinking of the fame that sometimes comes to men who discover a new thing, and of a Chair I might sit in at the University if I added one bright unheard-of piece of the shadowy mosaic of Martian history. I had had my share of wine and a bit more. That Chair looked a mile high and made of gold.

The stranger said softly, "I go from place to place in this wallow of Barrakesh and everywhere it is the same. I have ceased to be." His white teeth glittered for an instant in the shadow of the cowl. "They were wiser than I, my people. When Shandakor is dead, we are dead also, whether our bodies live or not."

"Shandakor?" I said. It had a sound of distant bells.

"How should an Earthman know? Yes, Shandakor! Ask of the men of Kesh and the men of Shun! Ask the kings of Mekh, who are half around the world! Ask of all the men of Mars—they have not forgotten Shandakor! But they will not tell you. It is a bitter shame to them, the memory and the name."

He stared out across the turbulent throng that filled the room and flowed over to the noisy street outside. "And I am here among them—lost."

"Shandakor is dead?"

"Dying. There were three of us who did not want to die. We came south across the desert—one turned back, one perished in the sand, I am here in Barrakesh." The metal of the wine cup bent between his hands.

I said, "And you regret your coming."

"I should have stayed and died with Shandakor. I know that now. But I cannot go back."

"Why not?" *I was thinking how the name John Ross would look, inscribed in golden letters on the scroll of the discoverers.*

"The desert is wide, Earthman. Too wide for one alone."

And I said, "I have a caravan. I am going north tonight."

A light came into his eyes, so strange and deadly that I was afraid. "No," he whispered. "*No!*"

I sat in silence, looking out across the crowd that had forgotten me as well, because I sat with the stranger. *A new race, an unknown city. And I was drunk.*

After a long while the stranger asked me, "What does an Earthman want in Shandakor?"

I told him. He laughed. "You study men," he said and laughed again, so that the red cloak rippled.

"If you want to go back I'll take you. If you don't, tell me where the city lies and I'll find it. Your race, your city, should have their place in history."

He said nothing but the wine had made me very shrewd and I could guess at what was going on in the stranger's mind. I got up.

"Consider it," I told him. "You can find me at the serai by the northern gate until the lesser moon is up. Then I'll be gone."

"Wait." His fingers fastened on my wrist. They hurt. I looked into his face and I did not like what I saw there. But, as Kardak had mentioned, I was not given much to wisdom.

The stranger said, "Your men will not go beyond the Wells of Karthedon."

"Then we'll go without them."

A long long silence. Then he said, "So be it."

I knew what he was thinking as plainly as though he had spoken the words. He was thinking that I was only an Earthman and that he would kill me when we came in sight of Shandakor.

II

THE CARAVAN tracks branch off at the Wells of Karthedon. One goes westward into Shun and one goes north through the passes of Outer Kesh. But there is a third one, more ancient than the others. It goes toward the east and it is never used. The deep rock wells are dry and the stone-built shelters have vanished under the rolling dunes. It is not until the track begins to climb the mountains that there are even memories.

Kardak refused politely to go beyond the Wells. He would wait for me, he said, a certain length of time, and if I came back we would go on into Shun. If I didn't—well, his full pay was left in charge of the local headman. He would collect it and go home. He had not liked having the stranger with us. He had doubled his price.

In all that long march up from Barrakesh I had not been able to get a word out of Kardak or the men concerning Shandakor. The stranger had not spoken either. He had told me his name—Corin—and nothing more. Cloaked and cowled he rode alone and brooded. His private devils were still with him and he had a new one now—impatience. He would have ridden us all to death if I had let him.

So Corin and I went east alone from Karthedon, with

75

two led animals and all the water we could carry. And now I could not hold him back.

"There is no time to stop," he said. "The days are running out. There is no time!"

When we reached the mountains we had only three animals left and when we crossed the first ridge we were afoot and leading the one remaining beast which carried the dwindling water skins.

We were following a road now. Partly hewn and partly worn it led up and over the mountains, those naked leaning mountains that were full of silence and peopled only with the shapes of red rock that the wind had carved.

"Armies used to come this way," said Corin. "Kings and caravans and beggars and human slaves, singers and dancing girls and the embassies of princes. This was the road to Shandakor."

The beast fell in a slide of rock and broke its neck and we carried the last water skin between us. It was not a heavy burden. It grew lighter and then was almost gone.

One afternoon, long before sunset, Corin said abruptly, "We will stop here."

The road went steeply up before us. There was nothing to be seen or heard. Corin sat down in the drifted dust. I crouched down too, a little distance from him. I watched him. His face was hidden and he did not speak.

The shadows thickened in that deep and narrow way. Overhead the strip of sky flared saffron and then red—and then the bright cruel stars came out. The wind worked at its cutting and polishing of stone, muttering to itself, an old and senile wind full of dissatisfaction and complaint. There was the dry faint click of falling pebbles.

The gun felt cold in my hand, covered with my cloak. I did not want to use it. But I did not want to die here on this silent pathway of vanished armies and caravans and kings.

A shaft of greenish moonlight crept down between the walls. Corin stood up.

"Twice now I have followed lies. Here I am met at last by truth."

I said, "I don't understand you."

"I thought I could escape the destruction. That was a lie.

76

Then I thought I could return to share it. That too was a lie. Now I see the truth. Shandakor is dying. I fled from that dying, which is the end of the city and the end of my race. The shame of flight is on me and I can never go back."

"What will you do?"

"I will die here."

"And I?"

"Did you think," asked Corin softly, "that I would bring an alien creature in to watch the end of Shandakor?"

I moved first. I didn't know what weapons he might have, hidden under that dark red cloak. I threw myself over on the dusty rock. Something went past my head with a hiss and a rattle and a flame of light and then I cut the legs from under him and he fell down forward and I got on top of him, very fast.

He had vitality. I had to hit his head twice against the rock before I could take out of his hands the vicious little instrument of metal rods. I threw it far away. I could not feel any other weapons on him except a knife and I took that, too. Then I got up.

I said, "I will carry you to Shandakor."

He lay still, draped in the tumbled folds of his cloak. His breath made a harsh sighing in his throat. "So be it." And then he asked for water.

I went to where the skin lay and picked it up, thinking that there was perhaps a cupful left. I didn't hear him move. What he did was done very silently with a sharp-edged ornament. I brought him the water and it was already over. I tried to lift him up. His eyes looked at me with a curiously brilliant look. Then he whispered three words, in a language I didn't know, and died. I let him down again.

His blood had poured out across the dust. And even in the moonlight I could see that it was not the color of human blood.

I crouched there for a long while, overcome with a strange sickness. Then I reached out and pushed that red cowl back to bare his head. It was a beautiful head. I had never seen it. If I had, I would not have gone alone with Corin into the mountains. I would have understood many things if I had seen it and not for fame nor money would I have gone to Shandakor.

His skull was narrow and arched and the shaping of the bones was very fine. On that skull was a covering of short curling fibers that had an almost metallic luster in the moonlight, silvery and bright. They stirred under my hand, soft silken wires responding of themselves to an alien touch. And even as I took my hand away the luster faded from them and the texture changed.

When I touched them again they did not stir. Corin's ears were pointed and there were silvery tufts on the tips of them. On them and on his forearms and his breast were the faint, faint memories of scales, a powdering of shining dust across the golden skin. I looked at his teeth and they were not human either.

I knew now why Corin had laughed when I told him that I studied men.

It was very still. I could hear the falling of pebbles and the little stones that rolled all lonely down the cliffs and the shift and whisper of dust in the settling cracks. The Wells of Karthedon were far away. Too far by several lifetimes for one man on foot with a cup of water.

I looked at the road that went steep and narrow on ahead. I looked at Corin. The wind was cold and the shaft of moonlight was growing thin. I did not want to stay alone in the dark with Corin.

I rose and went on along the road that led to Shandakor.

It was a long climb but not a long way. The road came out between two pinnacles of rock. Below that gateway, far below in the light of the little low moons that pass so swiftly over Mars, there was a mountain valley.

Once around that valley there were great peaks crowned with snow and crags of black and crimson where the flying lizards nested, the hawk-lizards with the red eyes. Below the crags there were forests, purple and green and gold, and a black tarn deep on the valley floor. But when I saw it, it was dead. The peaks had fallen away and the forests were gone and the tarn was only a pit in the naked rock.

In the midst of that desolation stood a fortress city.

There were lights in it, soft lights of many colors. The outer walls stood up, black and massive, a barrier against the creeping dust, and within them was an island of life.

The high towers were not ruined. The lights burned among them and there was movement in the streets.

A living city—and Corin had said that Shandakor was almost dead.

A rich and living city. I did not understand. But I knew one thing. Those who moved along the distant streets of Shandakor were not human.

I stood shivering in that windy pass. The bright towers of the city beckoned and there was something unnatural about all light life in the deathly valley. And then I thought that human or not the people of Shandakor might sell me water and a beast to carry it and I could get away out of these mountains, back to the Wells.

The road broadened, winding down the slope. I walked in the middle of it, not expecting anything. And suddenly two men came out of nowhere and barred the way.

I yelled. I jumped backward with my heart pounding and the sweat pouring off me. I saw their broadswords glitter in the moonlight. And they laughed.

They were human. One was a tall red barbarian from Mekh, which lay to the east half around Mars. The other was a leaner browner man from Taarak, which was farther still. I was scared and angry and astonished and I asked a foolish question.

"What are you doing *here?*"

"We wait," said the man of Taarak. He made a circle with his arm to take in all the darkling slopes around the valley. "From Kesh and Shun, from all the countries of the Norlands and the Marches men have come, to wait. And you?"

"I'm lost," I said. "I'm an Earthman and I have no quarrel with anyone." I was still shaking but now it was with relief. I would not have to go to Shandakor. If there was a barbarian army gathered here it must have supplies and I could deal with them.

I told them what I needed. "I can pay for them, pay well."

They looked at each other.

"Very well. Come and you can bargain with the chief."

They fell in on either side of me. We walked three paces and then I was on my face in the dirt and they were all over me like two great wildcats. When they were finished

79

they had everything I owned except the few articles of clothing for which they had no use. I got up again, wiping the blood from my mouth.

"For an outlander," said the man of Mekh, "you fight well." He chinked my money-bag up and down in his palm, feeling the weight of it, and then he handed me the leather bottle that hung at his side. "Drink," he told me. "That much I can't deny you. But our water must be carried a long way across these mountains and we have none to waste on Earthmen."

I was not proud. I emptied his bottle for him. And the man of Tarak said, smiling, "Go on to Shandakor. Perhaps they will give you water."

"But you've taken all my money!"

"They are rich in Shandakor. They don't need money. Go ask them for water."

They stood there, laughing at some secret joke of their own, and I did not like the sound of it. I could have killed them both and danced on their bodies but they had left me nothing but my bare hands to fight with. So presently I turned and went on and left them grinning in the dark behind me.

The road led down and out across the plain. I could feel eyes watching me, the eyes of the sentinels on the rounding slopes, piercing the dim moonlight. The walls of the city began to rise higher and higher. They hid everything but the top of one tall tower that had a queer squat globe on top of it. Rods of crystal projected from the globe. It revolved slowly and the rods sparkled with a sort of white fire that was just on the edge of seeing.

A causeway lifted toward the Western Gate. I mounted it, going very slowly, not wanting to go at all. And now I could see that the gate was open. *Open*—and this was a city under siege!

I stood still for some time, trying to puzzle out what meaning this might have—an army that did not attack and a city with open gates. I could not find a meaning. There were soldiers on the walls but they were lounging at their ease under the bright banners. Beyond the gate many people moved about but they were intent on their own affairs. I could not hear their voices.

I crept closer, closer still. Nothing happened. The sentries did not challenge me and no one spoke.

You know how necessity can force a man against his judgment and against his will?

I entered Shandakor.

III

THERE WAS an open space beyond the gate, a square large enough to hold an army. Around its edges were the stalls of merchants. Their canopies were of rich woven stuffs and the wares they sold were such things as have not been seen on Mars for more centuries than men can remember.

There were fruits and rare furs, the long-lost dyes that never fade, furnishings carved from varnished woods. There were spices and wines and exquisite cloths. In one place a merchant from the far south offered a ceremonial rug woven from the long bright hair of virgins. And it was new.

These merchants were all human. The nationalities of some of them I knew. Others I could guess at from traditional accounts. Some were utterly unknown.

Of the throngs that moved about among the stalls, quite a number were human also. There were merchant princes come to barter and there were companies of slaves on their way to the auction block. But the others . . .

I stayed where I was, pressed into a shadowy corner by the gate, and the chill that was on me was not all from the night wind.

The gold-skinned silver-crested lords of Shandakor I knew well enough from Corin. I say lords because that is how they bore themselves, walking proudly in their own place, attended by human slaves. And the humans who were not slaves made way for them and were most deferential as though they knew that they were greatly favored to be allowed inside the city at all. The women of Shandakor were very beautiful, slim golden sprites with their bright eyes and pointed ears.

And there were others. Slender creatures with great wings, some who were lithe and furred, some who were hairless and ugly and moved with a sinuous gliding, some so strangely shaped and colored that I could not even guess at their possible evolution.

The lost races of Mars. The ancient races, of whose pride and power nothing was left but the half-forgotten tales of old men in the farthest corners of the planet. Even I, who had made the anthropological history of Mars my business, had never heard of them except as the distorted shapes of legend, as satyrs and giants used to be known on Earth.

Yet here they were in gorgeous trappings, served by naked humans whose fetters were made of precious metals. And before them too the merchants drew aside and bowed.

The lights burned, many-colored—not the torches and cressets of the Mars I knew but cool radiances that fell from crystal globes. The walls of the buildings that rose around the marketplace were faced with rare veined marbles and the fluted towers that crowned them were inlaid with turquoise and cinnabar, with amber and jade and the wonderful corals of the southern oceans.

The splendid robes and the naked bodies moved in a swirling pattern about the square. There was buying and selling and I could see the mouths of the people open and shut. The mouths of the women laughed. But in all that crowded place there was no sound. No voice, no scuff of sandal, no clink of mail. There was only silence, the utter stillness of deserted places.

I began to understand why there was no need to shut the gates. No superstitious barbarian would venture himself into a city peopled by living phantoms.

And I—I was civilized. I was, in my nonmechanical way, a scientist. And had I not been trapped by my need for water and supplies I would have run away right out of the valley. But I had no place to run to and so I stayed and sweated and gagged on the acrid taste of fear.

What were these creatures that made no sound? Ghosts—images—dreams? The human and the nonhuman, the ancient, the proud, the lost and forgotten who were so insanely present—did they have some subtle form of life I knew nothing about? Could they see me as I saw them? Did they have thought and volition of their own?

It was the solidity of them, the intense and perfectly prosaic business in which they were engaged. Ghosts do not barter. They do not hang jeweled necklets upon their women nor argue about the price of a studded harness.

The solidity and the silence—that was the worst of it. If there had been one small living sound . . .

A dying city, Corin had said. *The days are running out.* What if they had run out? What if I were here in this massive pile of stone with all its countless rooms and streets and galleries and hidden ways, alone with the lights and the soundless phantoms?

Pure terror is a nasty thing. I had it then.

I began to move, very cautiously, along the wall. I wanted to get away from that marketplace. One of the hairless gliding nonhumans was bartering for a female slave. The girl was shrieking. I could see every drawn muscle in her face, the spasmodic working of her throat. Not the faintest sound came out.

I found a street that paralleled the wall. I went along it, catching glimpses of people—human people—inside the lighted buildings. Now and then men passed me and I hid from them. There was still no sound. I was careful how I set my feet. Somehow I had the idea that if I made a noise something terrible would happen.

A group of merchants came toward me. I stepped back into an archway and suddenly from behind me there came three spangled women of the serais. I was caught.

I did not want those silent laughing women to touch me. I leaped back toward the street and the merchants paused, turning their heads. I thought that they had seen me. I hesitated and the women came on. Their painted eyes shone and their red lips glistened. The ornaments on their bodies flashed. They walked straight into me.

I made noise then, all I had in my lungs. And the women passed through me. They spoke to the merchants and the merchants laughed. They went off together down the street. They hadn't seen me. They hadn't heard me. And when I got in their way I was no more than a shadow. They passed through me.

I sat down on the stones of the street and tried to think. I sat for a long time. Men and women walked through me as through the empty air. I sought to remember any sudden pain, as of an arrow in the back that might have killed me between two seconds, so that I hadn't known about it. It seemed more likely that I should be the ghost than the other way around.

I couldn't remember. My body felt solid to my hands as did the stones I sat on. They were cold and finally the cold got me up and sent me on again. There was no reason to hide any more. I walked down the middle of the street and I got used to not turning aside.

I came to another wall, running at right angles back into the city. I followed that and it curved around gradually until I found myself back at the marketplace, at the inner end of it. There was a gateway, with the main part of the city beyond it, and the wall continued. The nonhumans passed back and forth through the gate but no human did except the slaves. I realized then that all this section was a ghetto for the humans who came to Shandakor with the caravans.

I remembered how Corin had felt about me. And I wondered—granted that I were still alive and that some of the people of Shandakor were still on the same plane as myself —how they would feel about me if I trespassed in their city.

There was a fountain in the marketplace. The water sprang up sparkling in the colored light and filled a wide basin of carved stone. Men and women were drinking from it. I went to the fountain but when I put my hands in it all I felt was a dry basin filled with dust. I lifted my hands and let the dust trickle from them. I could see it clearly. But I saw the water too. A child leaned over and splashed it and it wetted the garments of the people. They struck the child and he cried and there was no sound.

I went on through the gate that was forbidden to the human race.

The avenues were wide. There were trees and flowers, wide parks and garden villas, great buildings as graceful as they were tall. A wise proud city, ancient in culture but not decayed, as beautiful as Athens but rich and strange, with a touch of the alien in every line of it. Can you think what it was like to walk in that city, among the silent throngs that were not human—to see the glory of it, that was not human either?

The towers of jade and cinnabar, the golden minarets, the lights and the colored silks, the enjoyment and the strength. And the people of Shandakor! No matter how far their souls have gone they will never forgive me.

How long I wandered I don't know. I had almost lost my fear in wonder at what I saw. And then, all at once in that deathly stillness, I heard a sound—the quick, soft scuffing of sandaled feet.

IV

I STOPPED where I was, in the middle of a plaza. The tall silver-crested ones drank wine under canopies of dusky blooms and in the center a score of winged girls as lovely as swans danced a slow strange measure that was more like flight than dancing. I looked all around. There were many people. How could you tell which one had made a noise?

Silence.

I turned and ran across the marble paving. I ran hard and then suddenly I stopped again, listening. *Scuff-scuff*—no more than a whisper, very light and swift. I spun around but it was gone. The soundless people walked and the dancers wove and shifted, spreading their white wings.

Someone was watching me. Some one of those indifferent shadows was not a shadow.

I went on. Wide streets led off from the plaza. I took one of them. I tried the trick of shifting pace, and two or three times I caught the echo of other steps than mine. Once I knew it was deliberate. Whoever followed me slipped silently among the noiseless crowd, blending with them, protected by them, only making a show of footsteps now and then to goad me.

I spoke to that mocking presence. I talked to it and listened to my own voice ringing hollow from the walls. The groups of people ebbed and flowed around me and there was no answer.

I tried making sudden leaps here and there among the passersby with my arms outspread. But all I caught was empty air. I wanted a place to hide and there was none.

The street was long. I went its length and the someone

85

followed me. There were many buildings, all lighted and populous and deathly still. I thought of trying to hide in the buildings but I could not bear to be closed in between walls with those people who were not people.

I came into a great circle, where a number of avenues met around the very tall tower I had seen with the revolving globe on top of it. I hesitated, not knowing which way to go. Someone was sobbing and I realized that it was myself, laboring to breathe. Sweat ran into the corners of my mouth and it was cold, and bitter.

A pebble dropped at my feet with a brittle *click*.

I bolted out across the square. Four or five times, without reason, like a rabbit caught in the open, I changed course and fetched up with my back against an ornamental pillar. From somewhere there came a sound of laughter.

I began to yell. I don't know what I said. Finally I stopped and there was only the silence and the passing throngs, who did not see nor hear me. And now it seemed to me that the silence was full of whispers just below the threshold of hearing.

A second pebble clattered off the pillar above my head. Another stung my body. I sprang away from the pillar. There was laughter and I ran.

There were infinites of streets, all glowing with color. There were many faces, strange faces, and robes blown out on a night wind, litters with scarlet curtains and beautiful cars like chariots drawn by beasts. They flowed past me like smoke, without sound, without substance, and the laughter pursued me, and I ran.

Four men of Shandakor came toward me. I plunged through them *but their bodies opposed mine, their hands caught me and I could see their eyes, their black shining eyes, looking at me. . . .*

I struggled briefly and then it was suddenly very dark.

The darkness caught me up and took me somewhere. Voices talked far away. One of them was a light young shiny sort of voice. It matched the laughter that had haunted me down the streets. I hated it.

I hated it so much that I fought to get free of the black river that was carrying me. There was a vertiginous whirling of light and sound and stubborn shadow and then things steadied down and I was ashamed of myself for having passed out.

I was in a room. It was fairly large, very beautiful, very old, the first place I had seen in Shandakor that showed real age—Martian age, that runs back before history had begun on Earth. The floor, of some magnificent somber stone the color of a moonless night, and the pale slim pillars that upheld the arching roof all showed the hollowings and smoothnesses of centuries. The wall paintings had dimmed and softened and the rugs that burned in pools of color on that dusky floor were worn as thin as silk.

There were men and women in that room, the alien folk of Shandakor. But these breathed and spoke and were alive. One of them, a girl-child with slender thighs and little pointed breasts, leaned against a pillar close beside me. Her black eyes watched me, full of dancing lights. When she saw that I was awake again she smiled and flicked a pebble at my feet.

I got up. I wanted to get that golden body between my hands and make it scream. And she said in High Martian, "Are you a human? I have never seen one before close to."

A man in a dark robe said, "Be still, Duani." He came and stood before me. He did not seem to be armed but others were and I remembered Corin's little weapon. I got hold of myself and did none of the things I wanted to do.

"What are you doing here?" asked the man in the dark robe.

I told him about myself and Corin, omitting only the fight that he and I had had before he died, and I told him how the hillmen had robbed me.

"They sent me here," I finished, "to ask for water."

Someone made a harsh humorless sound. The man before me said, "They were in a jesting mood."

"Surely you can spare some water and a beast!"

"Our beasts were slaughtered long ago. And as for water . . ." He paused, then asked bitterly, "Don't you understand? We are dying here of thirst!"

I looked at him and at the she-imp called Duani and the others. "You don't show any signs of it," I said.

"You saw how the human tribes have gathered like wolves upon the hills. What do you think they wait for? A year

87

ago they found and cut the buried aqueduct that brought water into Shandakor from the polar cap. All they needed then was patience. And their time is very near. The store we had in the cisterns is almost gone."

A certain anger at their submissiveness made me say, "Why do you stay here and die like mice bottled up in a jar? You could have fought your way out. I've seen your weapons."

"Our weapons are old and we are very few. And suppose that some of us did survive—tell me again, Earthman, how did Corin fare in the world of men?" He shook his head. "Once we were great and Shandakor was mighty. The human tribes of half a world paid tribute to us. We are only the last poor shadow of our race but we will not beg from men!"

"Besides," said Duani softly, "where else could we live but in Shandakor?"

"What about the others?" I asked. "The silent ones."

"They are the past," said the dark-robed man and his voice rang like a distant flare of trumpets.

Still I did not understand. I did not understand at all. But before I could ask more questions a man came up and said, "Rhul, he will have to die."

The tufted tips of Duani's ears quivered and her crest of silver curls came almost erect.

"No, Rhul!" she cried. "At least not right away."

There was a clamor from the others, chiefly in a rapid angular speech that must have predated all the syllables of men. And the one who had spoken before to Rhul repeated, "He will have to die! He has no place here. And we can't spare water."

"I'll share mine with him," said Duani, "for awhile."

I didn't want any favors from her and said so. "I came here after supplies. You haven't any, so I'll go away again. It's as simple as that." I couldn't buy from the barbarians, but I might make shift to steal.

Rhul shook his head. "I'm afraid not. We are only a handful. For years our single defense has been the living ghosts of our past who walk the streets, the shadows who man the walls. The barbarians believe in enchantments. If you were to enter Shandakor and leave it again alive the barbarians would know that the enchantment cannot kill. They would not wait any longer."

Angrily, because I was afraid, I said, "I can't see what difference that would make. You're going to die in a short while anyway."

"But in our own way, Earthman, and in our own time. Perhaps, being human, you can't understand that. It is a question of pride. The oldest race of Mars will end well, as it began."

He turned away with a small nod of the head that said *kill him*—as easily as that. And I saw the ugly little weapons rise.

V

THERE WAS a split second then that seemed like a year. I thought of many things but none of them were any good. It was a devil of a place to die without even a human hand to help me under. And then Duani flung her arms around me.

"You're all so full of dying and big thoughts!" she yelled at them. "And you're all paired off or so old you can't do anything but think! What about *me?* I don't have anyone to talk to and I'm sick of wandering alone, thinking how I'm going to die! Let me have him just for a little while? I told you I'd share my water."

On Earth a child might talk that way about a stray dog. And it is written in an old Book that a live dog is better than a dead lion. I hoped they would let her keep me.

They did. Rhul looked at Duani with a sort of weary compassion and lifted his hand. "Wait," he said to the men with the weapons. "I have thought how this human may be useful to us. We have so little time left now that it is a pity to waste any of it, yet much of it must be used up in tending the machine. He could do that labor—and a man can keep alive on very little water."

The others thought that over. Some of them dissented violently, not so much on the grounds of water as that it was unthinkable that a human should intrude on the last days of Shandakor. Corin had said the same thing. But Rhul was an old man. The tufts of his pointed ears were colorless as glass and his face was graven deep with years, and wisdom had distilled in him its bitter brew.

"A human of our own world, yes. But this man is of Earth and the men of Earth will come to be the new rulers of Mars as we were the old. And Mars will love them no better than she did us because they are as alien as we. So it is not unfitting that he should see us out."

They had to be content with that. I think they were already so close to the end that they did not really care. By ones and twos they left as though already they had wasted too much time away from the wonders that there were in the streets outside. Some of the men still held the weapons on me and others went and brought precious chains such as the human slaves had worn—shackles, so that I should not escape. They put them on me and Duani laughed.

"Come," said Rhul, "and I will show you the machine."

He led me from the room and up a winding stair. There were tall embrasures and looking through them I discovered that we were in the base of the very high tower with the globe. They must have carried me back to it after Duani had chased me with her laughter and her pebbles. I looked out over the glowing streets, so full of splendor and of silence, and asked Rhul why there were no ghosts inside the tower.

"You have seen the globe with the crystal rods?"

"Yes."

"We are under the shadow of its core. There had to be some retreat for us into reality. Otherwise we would lose the meaning of the dream."

The winding stair went up and up. The chain between my ankles clattered musically. Several times I tripped on it and fell.

"Never mind," Duani said. "You'll grow used to it."

We came at last into a circular room high in the tower. And I stopped and stared.

Most of the space in that room was occupied by a web of metal girders that supported a great gleaming shaft. The shaft disappeared upward through the roof. It was not tall but very massive, revolving slowly and quietly. There were traps, presumably for access to the offset shaft and the cogs that turned it. A ladder led to a trap in the roof.

All the visible metal was sound with only a little surface corrosion. What the alloy was I don't know and when I asked Rhul he only smiled rather sadly. "Knowledge is found," he said, "only to be lost again. Even we of Shandakor forget."

Every bit of that enormous structure had been shaped and polished and fitted into place by hand. Nearly all the Martian peoples work in metal. They seem to have a genius for it and while they are not and apparently never have been mechanical, as some of our races are on Earth, they find many uses for metal that we have never thought of.

But this before me was certainly the high point of the metalworkers' craft. When I saw what was down below, the beautifully simple power plant and the rotary drive setup with fewer moving parts than I would have thought possible, I was even more respectful. "How old is it?" I asked and again Rhul shook his head.

"Several thousand years ago there is a record of the yearly Hosting of the Shadows and it was not the first." He motioned me to follow him up the ladder, bidding Duani sternly to remain where she was. She came anyway.

There was a railed platform open to the universe and directly above it swung the mighty globe with its crystal rods that gleamed so strangely. Shandakor lay beneath us, a tapestry of many colors, bright and still, and out along the dark sides of the valley the tribesmen waited for the light to die.

"When there is no one left to tend the machine it will stop in time and then the men who have hated us so long will take what they want of Shandakor. Only fear has kept them out this long. The riches of half a world flowed through these streets and much of it remained."

He looked up at the globe. "Yes," he said, "we had knowledge. More, I think, than any other race of Mars."

"But you wouldn't share it with the humans."

Rhul smiled. "Would you give little children weapons to destroy you? We gave men better plowshares and brighter ornaments and if they invented a machine we did not take it from them. But we did not tempt and burden them with knowledge that was not their own. They were content to make war with sword and spear and so they had more

91

pleasure and less killing and the world was not torn apart."

"And you—how did you make war?"

"We defended our city. The human tribes had nothing that we coveted, so there was no reason to fight them except in self-defense. When we did we won." He paused. "The other nonhuman races were more stupid or less fortunate. They perished long ago.

He turned again to his explanations of the machine. "It draws its power directly from the sun. Some of the solar energy is converted and stored within the globe to serve as the light source. Some is sent down to turn the shaft."

"What if it should stop," Duani said, "while we're still alive?" She shivered, looking out over the beautiful streets.

"It won't—not if the Earthman wishes to live."

"What would I have to gain by stopping it?" I demanded.

"Nothing. And that," said Rhul, "is why I trust you. As long as the globe turns you are safe from the barbarians. After we are gone you will have the pick of the loot of Shandakor."

How I was going to get away with it afterward he did not tell me.

He motioned me down the ladder again but I asked him. "What *is* the globe, Rhul? How does it make the—the Shadows?"

He frowned. "I can only tell you what has become, I'm afraid, mere traditional knowledge. Our wise men studied deeply into the properties of light. They learned that light has a definite effect upon solid matter and they believe, because of that effect, that stone and metal and crystalline things retain a 'memory' of all that they have 'seen.' Why this should be I do not know."

I didn't try to explain to him the quantum theory and the photoelectric effect nor the various experiments of Einstein and Millikan and the men who followed them. I didn't know them well enough myself and the old High Martian is deficient in such terminology.

I only said, "The wise men of my world also know that the impact of light tears away tiny particles from the substance it strikes."

I was beginning to get a glimmering of the truth. Light patterns "cut" in the electrons of metal and stone—sound patterns cut in unlikely-looking mediums of plastic, each needing only the proper "needle" to recreate the recorded melody or the recorded picture.

"They constructed the globe," said Rhul. "I do not know how many generations that required nor how many failures they must have had. But they found at last the invisible light that makes the stones give up their memories."

In other words they had found their needle. What wavelength in the electromagnetic spectrum flowed out from those crystal rods, there was no way for me to know. But where they probed the walls and the paving blocks of Shandakor they scanned the hidden patterns that were buried in them and brought them forth again in form and color—as the electron needle brings forth whole symphonies from a little ridged disc.

How they had achieved sequence and selectivity was another matter. Rhul said something about the "memories" having different lengths. Perhaps he meant depth of penetration. The stones of Shandakor were ages old and the outer surfaces would have worn away. The earliest impressions would be gone altogether or at least have become fragmentary and extremely shallow.

Perhaps the scanning beams could differentiate between the overlapping layers of impressions by that fraction of a micron difference in depth. Photons only penetrate so far into any given substance but if that substance is constantly growing less in thickness the photons would have the effect of going deeper. I imagine the globe was accurate in centuries or numbers of centuries, not in years.

However it was, the Shadows of a golden past walked the streets of Shandakor and the last men of the race waited quietly for death, remembering their glory.

Rhul took me below again and showed me what my tasks would be, chiefly involving a queer sort of lubricant and a careful watch over the power leads. I would have to spend most of my time there but not all of it. During the free periods, Duani might take me where she would.

The old man went away. Duani leaned herself against a girder and studied me with intense interest. "How are you called?" she asked.

"John Ross."

"JonRoss," she repeated and smiled. She began to walk around me, touching my hair, inspecting my arms and chest, taking a child's delight in discovering all the differences there were between herself and what we call a human. And that was the beginning of my captivity.

VI

THERE WERE days and nights, scant food and scanter water. There was Duani. And there was Shandakor. I lost my fear. And whether I lived to occupy the Chair or not, this was something to have seen.

Duani was my guide. I was tender of my duties because my neck depended on them but there was time to wander in the streets, to watch the crowded pageant that was not and sense the stillness and the desolation that were so cruelly real.

I began to get the feel of what this alien culture had been like and how it had dominated half a world without the need of conquest.

In a Hall of Government, built of white marble and decorated with wall friezes of austere magnificence, I watched the careful choosing and the crowning of a king. I saw the places of learning. I saw the young men trained for war as fully as they were instructed in the arts of peace. I saw the pleasure gardens, the theaters, the forums, the sporting fields—and saw the places of work, where the men and women of Shandakor coaxed beauty from their looms and forges to trade for the things they wanted from the human world.

The human slaves were brought by their own kind to be sold, and they seemed to be well treated, as one treats a useful animal in which one has invested money. They had their work to do but it was only a small part of the work of the city.

The things that could be had nowhere else on Mars—the tools, the textiles, the fine work in metal and precious stones, the glass and porcelain—were fashioned by the people of Shandakor and they were proud of their skill. Their scientific knowledge they kept entirely to themselves, except what concerned agriculture or medicine or better ways of building drains and houses.

They were the lawgivers, the teachers. And the humans took all they would give and hated them for it. How long it had taken these people to attain such a degree of civilization Duani could not tell me. Neither could old Rhul.

"It is certain that we lived in communities, had a form of civil government, a system of numbers and written speech, before the human tribes. There are traditions of an earlier race than ours, from whom we learned these things. Whether or not this is true I do not know."

In its prime Shandakor had been a vast and flourishing city with countless thousands of inhabitants. Yet I could see no signs of poverty or crime. I couldn't even find a prison.

"Murder was punishable by death," said Rhul, "but it was most infrequent. Theft was for slaves. We did not stoop to it." He watched my face, smiling a little acid smile. "That startles you—a great city without suffering or crime or places of punishment."

I had to admit that it did. "Elder race or not, how did you manage to do it? I'm a student of cultures, both here and on my own world. I know all the usual patterns of development and I've read all the theories about them—but Shandakor doesn't fit any of them."

Rhul's smile deepened. "You are human," he said. "Do you wish the truth?"

"Of course."

"Then I will tell you. We developed the faculty of reason."

For a moment I thought he was joking. "Come," I said, "man is a reasoning being—on Earth the only reasoning being."

"I do not know of Earth," he answered courteously. "But on Mars man has always said, 'I reason, I am above the beasts because I reason.' And he has been very proud of himself because he could reason. It is the mark of his humanity. Being convinced that reason operates automatically within him he orders his life and his government upon emotion and superstition.

"He hates and fears and believes, not with reason but because he is told to by other men or by tradition. He does one thing and says another and his reason teaches him no difference between fact and falsehood. His bloodiest wars are fought for the merest whim—and that is why we did not give him weapons. His greatest follies appear to him the highest wisdom, his basest betrayals become noble acts —and that is why we could not teach him justice. We learned to reason. Man only learned to talk."

I understood then why the human tribes had hated the men of Shandakor. I said angrily, "Perhaps that is so on Mars. But only reasoning minds can develop great technologies and we humans of Earth have outstripped yours a million times. All right, you know or knew some things we haven't learned yet, in optics and some branches of electronics and perhaps in metallurgy. But . . ."

I went on to tell him all the things we had that Shandakor did not. "You never went beyond the beast of burden and the simple wheel. We achieved flight long ago. We have conquered space and the planets. We'll go on to conquer the stars!"

Rhul nodded. "Perhaps we were wrong. We remained here and conquered ourselves." He looked out toward the slopes where the barbarian army waited and he sighed. "In the end it is all the same."

Days and nights and Duani, bringing me food, sharing her water, asking questions, taking me through the city. The only thing she would not show me was something they called the Place of Sleep. "I shall be there soon enough," she said and shivered.

"How long?" I asked. It was an ugly thing to say.

"We are not told. Rhul watches the level in the cisterns and when it's time . . ." She made a gesture with her hands. "Let us go up on the wall."

We went up among the ghostly soldiery and the phantom banners. Outside there were darkness and death and the coming of death. Inside there were light and beauty, the last proud blaze of Shandakor under the shadow of its doom. There was an eerie magic in it that had begun to tell on me. I watched Duani. She leaned against the parapet, looking outward. The wind ruffled her silver crest, pressed her garments close against her body. Her eyes were full of moonlight and I could not read them. Then I saw that there were tears.

I put my arm around her shoulders. She was only a child, an alien child, not of my race or breed. . . .

"JonRoss."

"Yes?"

"There are so many things I will never know."

It was the first time I had touched her. Those curious curls stirred under my fingers, warm and alive. The tips of her pointed ears were soft as a kitten's.

"Duani."

"What?"

"I don't know. . . ."

I kissed her. She drew back and gave me a startled look from those black brilliant eyes and suddenly I stopped thinking that she was a child and I forgot that she was not human and—I didn't care.

"Duani, listen. You don't have to go to the Place of Sleep."

She looked at me, her cloak spread out upon the night wind, her hands against my chest.

"There's a whole world out there to live in. And if you aren't happy there I'll take you to my world, to Earth. There isn't any reason why you have to die!"

Still she looked at me and did not speak. In the streets below the silent throngs went by and the towers glowed with many colors. Duani's gaze moved slowly to the darkness beyond the wall, to the barren valley and the hostile rocks.

"No."

"Why not? Because of Rhul, because of all this talk of pride and race?"

"Because of truth. Corin learned it."

I didn't want to think about Corin. "He was alone. You're not. You'd never be alone."

She brought her hands up and laid them on my cheeks very gently. "That green star, that is your world. Suppose it were to vanish and you were the last of all the men of Earth. Suppose you lived with me in Shandakor forever— would you not be alone?"

"It wouldn't matter if I had you."

She shook her head. "It would matter. And our two

races are as far apart as the stars. We would have nothing to share between us."

Remembering what Rhul had told me I flared up and said some angry things. She let me say them and then she smiled. "It is none of that, JonRoss." She turned to look out over the city. "This is my place and no other. When it is gone I must be gone too."

Quite suddenly I hated Shandakor.

I didn't sleep much after that. Every time Duani left me I was afraid she might never come back. Rhul would tell me nothing and I didn't dare to question him too much. The hours rushed by like seconds and Duani was happy and I was not. My shackles had magnetic locks. I couldn't break them and I couldn't cut the chains.

One evening Duani came to me with something in her face and in the way she moved that told me the truth long before I could make her put it into words. She clung to me, not wanting to talk, but at last she said, "Today there was a casting of lots and the first hundred have gone to the Place of Sleep."

"It is the beginning, then."

She nodded. "Every day there will be another hundred until all are gone."

I couldn't stand it any longer. I thrust her away and stood up. "You know where the 'keys' are. Get these chains off me!"

She shook her head. "Let us not quarrel now, JonRoss. Come. I want to walk in the city."

We had quarreled more than once, and fiercely. She would not leave Shandakor and I couldn't take her out by force as long as I was chained. And I was not to be released until everyone but Rhul had entered the Place of Sleep and the last page of that long history had been written.

I walked with her among the dancers and the slaves and the bright-cloaked princes. There were no temples in Shandakor. If they worshiped anything it was beauty and to that their whole city was a shrine. Duani's eyes were rapt and there was a remoteness in her now.

I held her hand and looked at the towers of turquoise and cinnabar, the pavings of rose quartz and marble, the walls of pink and white and deep red coral, and to me they were hideous. The ghostly crowds, the mockery of life, the phantom splendors of the past were hideous, a drug, a snare.

"The faculty of reason!" I thought and saw no reason in any of it.

I looked up to where the great globe turned and turned against the sky, keeping these mockeries alive. "Have you ever seen the city as it is—without the Shadows?"

"No. I think only Rhul, who is the oldest, remembers it that way. I think it must have been very lonely. Even then there were less than three thousand of us left."

It must indeed have been lonely. They must have wanted the Shadows as much to people the empty streets as to fend off the enemies who believed in magic.

I kept looking at the globe. We walked for a long time. And then I said, "I must go back to the tower."

She smiled at me very tenderly. "Soon you will be free of the tower—and of these." She touched the chains. "No, don't be sad, JonRoss. You will remember me and Shandakor as one remembers a dream." She held up her face, that was so lovely and so unlike the meaty faces of human women, and her eyes were full of somber lights. I kissed her and then I caught her up in my arms and carried her back to the tower.

In that room, where the great shaft turned, I told her, "I have to tend the things below. Go up onto the platform, Duani, where you can see all Shandakor. I'll be with you soon."

I don't know whether she had some hint of what was in my mind or whether it was only the imminence of parting that made her look at me as she did. I thought she was going to speak but she did not, climbing the ladder obediently. I watched her slender golden body vanish upward. Then I went into the chamber below.

There was a heavy metal bar there that was part of a manual control for regulating the rate of turn. I took it off its pin. Then I closed the simple switches on the power plant. I tore out all the leads and smashed the connections with the bar. I did what damage I could to the cogs and the offset shaft. I worked very fast. Then I went up into the main chamber again. The great shaft was still turning but slowly, ever more slowly.

There was a cry from above me and I saw Duani. I sprang up the ladder, thrusting her back onto the platform. The globe moved heavily of its own momentum. Soon it would stop but the white fires still flickered in the crystal rods. I climbed up onto the railing, clinging to a strut. The chains on my wrists and ankles made it hard but I could reach. Duani tried to pull me down. I think she was screaming. I hung on and smashed the crystal rods with the bar, as many as I could.

There was no more motion, no more light. I got down on the platform again and dropped the bar. Duani had forgotten me. She was looking at the city.

The lights of many colors that had burned there were burning still but they were old and dim, cold embers without radiance. The towers of jade and turquoise rose up against the little moons and they were broken and cracked with time and there was no glory in them. They were desolate and very sad. The night lay clotted around their feet. The streets, the plazas and the market squares were empty, their marble paving blank and bare. The soldiers had gone from the walls of Shandakor, with their banners and their bright mail, and there was no longer any movement anywhere within the gates.

Duani let out one small voiceless cry. And as though in answer to it, suddenly from the darkness of the valley and the slopes beyond there rose a thin fierce howling as of wolves.

"Why?" she whispered. "*Why?*" She turned to me. Her face was pitiful. I caught her to me.

"I couldn't let you die! Not for dreams and visions, nothing. Look, Duani. Look at Shandakor." I wanted to force her to understand. "Shandakor is broken and ugly and forlorn. It is a dead city—but you're alive. There are many cities but only one life for you."

Still she looked at me and it was hard to meet her eyes. She said, "We knew all that, JonRoss."

"Duani, you're a child; you've only a child's way of thought. Forget the past and think of tomorrow. We can get through the barbarians. Corin did. And after that . . ."

"And after that you would still be human—and I would not."

From below us in the dim and empty streets there came a sound of lamentation. I tried to hold her but she slipped out from between my hands. "And I am glad that you are human," she whispered. "You will never understand what you have done."

And she was gone before I could stop her, down into the tower.

I went after her. Down the endless winding stairs with my chains clattering between my feet, out into the streets, the dark and broken and deserted streets of Shandakor. I called her name and her golden body went before me, fleet and slender, distant and more distant. The chains dragged upon my feet and the night took her away from me.

I stopped. The whelming silence rushed smoothly over me and I was bitterly afraid of this dark dead Shandakor that I did not know. I called again to Duani and then I began to search for her in the shattered shadowed streets. I know now how long it must have been before I found her.

For when I found her, she was with the others. The last people of Shandakor, the men and the women, the women first, were walking silently in a long line toward a low flat-roofed building that I knew without telling was the Place of Sleep.

They were going to die and there was no pride in their faces now. There was a sickness in them, a sickness and a hurt in their eyes as they moved heavily forward, not looking, not wanting to look at the sordid ancient streets that I had stripped of glory.

"*Duani!*" I called, and ran forward but she did not turn in her place in the line. And I saw that she was weeping.

Rhul turned toward me, and his look had a weary contempt that was more bitter than a curse. "Of what use, after all, to kill you now?"

"But I did this thing! *I* did it!"

"You are only human."

The long line shuffled on and Duani's little feet were closer to that final doorway. Rhul looked upward at the

101

sky. "There is still time before the sunrise. The women at least will be spared the indignity of spears."

"Let me go with her!"

I tried to follow her, to take my place in line. And the weapon in Rhul's hand moved and there was the pain and I lay as Corin had lain while they went silently on into the Place of Sleep.

The barbarians found me when they came, still half doubtful, into the city after dawn. I think they were afraid of me. I think they feared me as a wizard who had somehow destroyed all the folk of Shandakor.

For they broke my chains and healed my wounds and later they even gave me out of the loot of Shandakor the only thing I wanted—a bit of porcelain, shaped like the head of a young girl.

I sit in the Chair that I craved at the University and my name is written on the roll of the discoverers. I am eminent, I am respectable—I, who murdered the glory of a race.

Why didn't I go after Duani into the Place of Sleep? I could have crawled! I could have dragged myself across those stones. And I wish to God I had. I wish that I had died with Shandakor!

2031: PURPLE PRIESTESS OF THE MAD MOON

IN THE observation bubble of the TSS *Goddard* Harvey Selden watched the tawny face of the planet grow. He could make out rose-red deserts where tiny sandstorms blew, and dark areas of vegetation like textured silk. Once or twice he caught the bright flash of water from one of the canals. He sat motionless, rapt and delighted. He had been afraid that this confrontation would offer very little to his emotions; he had since childhood witnessed innumerable identical approaches on the tri-di screen, which was almost the same as being there one's self. But the actuality had a flavor and imminence that he found immensely thrilling.

After all, an alien planet . . .

After all, *Mars* . . .

He was almost angry when he realized that Bentham had come into the bubble. Bentham was Third Officer and at his age this was an admission of failure. The reason for it, Selden thought, was stamped quite clearly on his face, and he felt sorry for Bentham as he felt sorry for anyone afflicted with alcoholism. Still, the man was friendly and he had seemed much impressed by Selden's knowledge of Mars. So Selden smiled and nodded.

"Quite a thrill," he said.

Bentham glanced at the onrushing planet. "It always is. You know anybody down there?"

"No. But after I check in with the Bureau . . .

"When will you do that?"

"Tomorrow. I mean, counting from after we land, of course . . . a little confusing, isn't it, this time thing?" He knew they did three or four complete orbits on a descending spiral, which meant three or four days and nights.

Bentham said, "But in the meantime, you don't know anybody."

Selden shook his head.

"Well," said Bentham, "I'm having dinner with some Martian friends. Why don't you come along? You might find it interesting."

"Oh," said Selden eagerly, "that would be . . . But are you sure your friends won't mind? I mean, an unexpected guest dragged in at the last minute . . ."

"They won't mind," Bentham said. "I'll give them plenty of warning. Where are you staying?"

"The Kahora-Hilton."

"Of course," said Bentham. "I'll pick you up around seven." He smiled. "Kahora time."

He went out, leaving Selden with some lingering qualms of doubt. Bentham was perhaps not quite the person he would have chosen to introduce him to Martian society. Still, he was an officer and could be presumed to be a gentleman. And he had been on the Mars run for a long time. Of course he would have friends, and what an unlooked-for and wonderful chance this was to go actually into a Martian home and visit with a Martian family. He was ashamed of his momentary uneasiness, and was able to analyze it quite quickly as being based in his own sense of insecurity, which of course arose from being faced with a totally unfamiliar environment. Once he had brought this negative attitude into the open it was easy to correct it. After a quarter of an hour of positive therapy he found himself hardly able to wait for the evening.

Kahora had grown in half a century. Originally, Selden knew, it had been founded as a Trade City under the infamous old Umbrella Treaty, so-called because it could be manipulated to cover anything, which had been concluded between the then World Government of Terra and the impoverished Martian Federation of City-States. At that time the city was housed under a single dome, climate-conditioned for the comfort of the outworld traders and politicians who frequented it and who were unused to the rigors of cold and thin-aired Mars. In addition to the climate, various other luxuries were installed in the Trade Cities, so that they had been compared with certain Biblical locales, and crimes of many different sorts, even murder, had been known to occur in them.

But all of that, or nearly all of that, was in the bad old days of *laissez-faire,* and now Kahora was the administrative capital of Mars, sheltered under a complex of eight shining domes. From the spaceport fifteen miles away, Selden saw the city as a pale shimmer of gossamer bubbles touched by the low sun. As the spaceport skimmer flew him across the intervening miles of red sand and dark green moss-grass, he saw the lights come on in the quick dusk and the buildings underneath the domes rose and took shape, clean and graceful and clothed in radiance. He thought that he had never seen anything so beautiful. From the landing stage inside one of the domes a silent battery-powered cab took him to his hotel along gracious streets, where the lights glowed and people of many races walked leisurely. The whole trip, from debarkation to hotel lobby, was accomplished in completely air-conditioned comfort, and Selden was not sorry. The landscape looked awfully bleak, and one needed only to glance at it to know that it was damnably cold. Just before the skimmer entered the airlock it crossed the Kahora canal, and the water looked like black ice. He knew that he might have to cope with all this presently, but he was not in any hurry.

Selden's room was pleasantly homelike and the view of the city was superb. He showered and shaved, dressed in his best dark silk, and then sat for a while on his small balcony overlooking the Triangle with the Three Worlds represented at its apices. The air he breathed was warm and faintly scented. The city sounds that rose to him were pleasantly subdued. He began to run over in his mind the rules he had learned for proper behavior in a Martian house, the ceremonial phrases and gestures. He wondered whether Bentham's friends would speak High or Low Martian. Low, probably, since that was most commonly in use with outsiders. He hoped his accent was not too barbarous. On the whole he felt adequate. He leaned back in his comfortable chair and found himself looking at the sky.

105

There were two moons in it, racing high above the glow and distortion of the dome. And for some reason, although he knew perfectly well that Mars had two moons, this bit of alienage had a powerful effect on him. For the first time he realized, not merely with his intellect but with his heart and bowels, that he was on a strange world a long, long way from home.

He went down to the bar to wait for Bentham.

The man arrived in good time, freshly turned out in civilian silks and, Selden was glad to see, perfectly sober. He bought him a drink and then followed him into a cab, which bore them quietly from the central dome into one of the outer ones.

"The original one," Bentham said. "It's chiefly residential now. The buildings are older, but very comfortable." They were halted at a concourse waiting for a flow of cross traffic to pass and Bentham pointed at the dome roof. "Have you seen the moons? They're both in the sky now. That's the thing people seem to notice the most when they first land."

"Yes," Selden said. "I've seen them. It is . . . uh . . . striking."

"The one we call Deimos . . . that one there . . . the Martian name is Vashna, of course . . . that's the one that in certain phases was called the Mad Moon."

"Oh no," Selden said. "That was Phobos. Denderon."

Bentham gave him a look and he reddened a bit. "I mean, I think it was." He knew damn well it was, but after all . . . "Of course you've been here many times, and I could be mistaken . . ."

Bentham shrugged. "Easy enough to settle it. We'll ask Mak."

"Who?"

"Firsa Mak. Our host."

"Oh," said Selden, "I wouldn't . . ."

But the cab sped on then and Bentham was pointing out some other thing of interest and the subject passed.

Almost against the outer curve of the dome there was a building of pale gold and the cab stopped there. A few minutes later Selden was being introduced to Firsa Mak.

He had met Martians before, but only rarely and never *in situ*. He was a dark, small, lean, catlike man with the most astonishing yellow eyes. The man wore the traditional white tunic of the Trade Cities, exotic and very graceful. A gold earring that Selden recognized as a priceless antique hung from his left earlobe. He was not at all like the rather round and soft Martians Selden had met on Terra. He flinched before those eyes, and the carefully mustered words of greeting stuck in his throat. Then there was no need for them as Firsa Mak shook his hand and said, "Hello. Welcome to Mars. Come on in."

A wiry brown hand propelled him in the most friendly fashion into a large low room with a glass wall that looked out through the dome at the moon-washed desert. The furniture was simple modern stuff and very comfortable, with here and there a bit of sculpture or a wall plaque as fine as, but no better than, the Martian handcrafts obtainable at the good specialty shops in N'York. On one of the couches a very long-legged Earthman sat drinking in a cloud of smoke. He was introduced as Altman. He had a face like old leather left too long in the sun, and he looked at Selden as from a great height and a far distance. Curled up beside him was a dark girl, or woman . . . Selden could not decide which because of the smoothness of her face and the too-great wisdom of her eyes, which were as yellow and unwinking as Firsa Mak's.

"My sister," Firsa Mak said. "Mrs. Altman. And this is Lella."

He did not say exactly who Lella was, and Selden did not at the moment care. She had just come in from the kitchen bearing a tray of something or other, and she wore a costume that Selden had read about but never seen. A length of brilliant silk, something between red and burnt orange, was wrapped about her hips and caught at the waist by a broad girdle. Below the skirt her slim brown ankles showed, with anklets of tiny golden bells that chimed faintly as she walked. Above the skirt her body was bare and splendidly made. A necklace of gold plaques intricately pierced and hammered circled her throat, and more of the tiny bells hung from her ears. Her hair was long and deeply black and her eyes were green, with the most enchanting tilt. She smiled at Selden, and moved away with her elfin music, and he stood stupidly staring after her, hardly aware that he had taken a glass of dark liquor from her proffered tray.

Presently Selden was sitting on some cushions between the Altmans and Firsa Mak, with Bentham opposite. Lella kept moving distractingly in and out, keeping their glasses filled with the peculiar smoky-tasting hellfire.

"Bentham tells me you're with the Bureau of Interworld Cultural Relations," Firsa Mak said.

"Yes," said Selden. Altman was looking at him with that strange remote glare, making him feel acutely uncomfortable.

"Ah. And what is your particular field?"

"Handcrafts. Metalwork. Uh . . . the ancient type of thing, like that. . . ." He indicated Lella's necklace, and she smiled.

"It is old," she said, and her voice was sweet as the chiming bells. "I would not even guess how old."

"The pierced pattern," Selden said, "is characteristic of the Seventeenth Dynasty of the Khalide Kings of Jekkara, which lasted for approximately two thousand years at the period when Jekkara was declining from her position as a maritime power. The sea was receding significantly then, say between fourteen and sixteen thousand years ago."

"So old?" Lella said, and fingered the necklace wonderingly.

"That depends," said Bentham. "Is it genuine, Lella, or is it a copy?"

Lella dropped to her knees beside Selden. "You will say."

They all waited. Selden began to sweat. He had studied hundreds of necklaces, but never *in situ*. Suddenly he was not sure at all whether the damned thing was genuine, and he was just as suddenly positive that they did know and were needling him. The plaques rose and fell gently to the lift of Lella's breathing. A faint dry spicy fragrance reached his nostrils. He touched the gold, lifted one of the plaques and felt of it, warm from her flesh, and yearned for a nice uncomplicated textbook that had diagrams and illustrations and nothing more to take your mind off your subject. He was tempted to tell them to go to hell. They were just waiting for him to make a mistake. Then he got madder and bolder and he put his whole hand under the collar, lifting it away from her neck and testing the weight of it. It was worn thin and light as tissue paper and the undersurface was still pocked by the ancient hammer strokes in the particular fashion of the Khalide artificers.

It was a terribly crude test, but his blood was up. He looked into the tilted green eyes and said authoritatively, "It's genuine."

"How wonderful that you know!" She caught his hand between hers and pressed it and laughed aloud with pleasure. "You have studied very long?"

"Very long." He felt good now. He hadn't let them get him down. The hellfire had worked its way up into his head, where it was buzzing gently, and Lella's attention was even more pleasantly intoxicating.

"What will you do now with this knowledge?" she asked.

"Well," he said, "as you know, so many of the ancient skills have been lost, and your people are looking for ways to expand their economy, so the Bureau is hoping to start a program to reeducate metalworkers in places like Jekkara and Valkis. . . ."

Altman said in a remote and very quiet voice, "Oh good God Albloodymighty."

Selden said, "I beg your pardon?"

"Nothing," Altman said. "Nothing."

Bentham turned to Firsa Mak. "By the way, Selden and I had a difference of opinion on the way here. He's probably right, but I said I'd ask you. . . ."

Selden said hastily, "Oh, let's forget it, Bentham." But Bentham was obtuse and insistent.

"The Mad Moon, Firsa Mak. I say Vashna, he says Denderon."

"Denderon, of course," said Firsa Mak, and looked at Selden. "So you know all about that, too."

"Oh," said Selden, embarrassed and annoyed with Bentham for bringing it up, "please, we thoroughly understand that that was all a mistake."

Altman leaned forward. "Mistake?"

"Certainly. The early accounts . . ." He looked at Firsa Mak and his sister and Lella and they all seemed to be waiting for him to go on, so he did, uncomfortably. "I mean, they resulted from distortions of folklore, misinterpretation of local customs, pure ignorance . . . in some cases, they were downright lies." He waved his hand deprecatingly. "We don't believe in the Rites of the Purple Priestess and all that nonsense. That is to say, we don't believe they ever *occurred*, really."

He hoped that would close the subject, but Bentham was determined to hang to it. "I've read eyewitness accounts, Selden."

"Fabrications. Traveler's tales. After all, the Earthmen who first came to Mars were strictly the piratical exploiter type and were hardly either qualified or reliable observers. . . ."

"They don't need us any more," said Altman softly, staring at Selden but not seeming to see him. "They don't need us at all." And he muttered something about winged pigs and the gods of the marketplace. Selden had a sudden horrid certainty that Altman was himself one of those early piratical exploiters and that he had irreparably insulted him.

And then Firsa Mak said with honest curiosity, "Why is it that all you young Earthmen are so ready to cry down the things your own people have done?"

Selden felt Altman's eyes upon him, but he was into this now and there was no backing down. He said with quiet dignity, "Because we feel that if our people have made mistakes we should be honest enough to admit them."

"A truly noble attitude," said Firsa Mak. "But about the Purple Priestess . . ."

"I assure you," said Selden hastily, "that old canard is long forgotten. The men who did the serious research, the anthropologists and sociologists who came after the . . . uh . . . the adventurers, were far better qualified to evaluate the data. They completely demolished the idea that the rites involved human sacrifice, and of course the monstrous Dark Lord the priestess was supposed to serve was merely the memory of an extremely ancient earth-god . . . mars-god, I should say, but you know what I mean, a primitive nature thing, like the sky or the wind."

Firsa Mak said gently, "But there was a rite . . ."

"Well, yes," said Selden, "undoubtedly. But the experts proved that it was purely vestigial, like . . . well, like our own children dancing around the Maypole."

110

"The Low Canallers," said Altman, "never danced around any Maypoles." He rose slowly and Selden watched him stretch higher and higher above him. He must have stood a good six inches over six feet, and even from that height his eyes pierced Selden. "How many of your qualified observers went into the hills above Jekkara?"

Selden began to bristle a bit. The feeling that for some reason he was being baited grew stronger. "You must know that until very recently the Low Canal towns were closed to Earthman. . . ."

"Except for a few adventurers."

"Who left highly dubious memoirs! And even yet you have to have a diplomatic passport involving miles of red tape, and you're allowed very little freedom of movement when you get there. But it *is* a beginning, and we hope, we hope very greatly, that we can persuade the Low Canallers to accept our friendship and assistance. It's a pity that their own secretiveness fostered such a bad image. For decades the only ideas we had of the Low Canal towns came from the lurid accounts of the early travelers, and the extremely biased—as we learned later—attitude of the City-States. We used to think of Jekkara and Valkis as, well, perfect sinks of iniquity. . . ."

Altman was smiling at him. "But, my dear boy," he said, "they are. They are."

Selden tried to disengage his hand from Lella's. He found that he could not, and it was about then that he began to be just the least little bit frightened.

"I don't understand," he said plaintively. "Did you get me here just to bait me? If you did, I don't think it's very . . . Bentham?"

Bentham was at the door. The door now seemed to be much farther away than Selden remembered and there was a kind of mist between him and it so that Bentham's figure was indistinct. Nevertheless he saw it raise a hand and heard it say, "Goodbye." Then it was gone, and Selden, feeling infinitely forlorn, turned to look into Lella's eyes. "I don't understand," he said. "I don't understand." Her eyes were green and enormous and deep without limit. He felt himself topple and fall giddily into the abyss, and then of course it was far too late to be afraid.

Hearing returned to him first, with the steady roar of jets, and then there was the bodily sensation of being borne through air that was shaken occasionally by large turbulences. He opened his eyes, in wild alarm. It was several minutes before he could see anything but a thick fog. The fog cleared gradually and he found himself staring at Lella's gold necklace and remembering with great clarity the information concerning it that he had rattled off so glibly and with such modest pride. A simple and obvious truth came to him.

"You're from Jekkara," he said, and only then did he realize that there was a gag in his mouth. Lella started and looked down at him.

"He's awake."

Firsa Mak rose and bent over Selden, examining the gag and a set of antique manacles that bound his wrists. Again Selden flinched from those fierce and brilliant eyes. Firsa Mak seemed to hesitate, on the verge of removing the gag, and Selden mustered his voice and courage to demand explanations. A buzzer sounded in the cabin, apparently a signal from the pilot, and at the same time the motion of the copter altered. Firsa Mak shook his head.

"Later, Selden. I have to leave you this way because I can't trust you, and all our lives are in danger, not just yours . . . though yours most of all." He leaned forward. "This is necessary, Selden. Believe me."

"Not necessary," Altman said, appearing stooped under the cabin ceiling. "Vital. You'll understand that, later."

Lella said harshly, "I wonder if he will."

"If he doesn't," Altman said, "God help them all, because no one else can."

Mrs. Altman came with a load of heavy cloaks. They had all changed their clothes since Selden had last seen them, except Lella, who had merely added an upper garment of native wool. Mrs. Altman now wore the Low Canal garb, and Firsa Mak had a crimson tunic held with a wide belt around his hips. Altman looked somehow incredibly right in the leather of a desert tribesman; he was too tall, Selden guessed, to pass for a Jekkaran. He wore the desert harness easily, as though he had worn it many times. They made Selden stand while they wrapped a cloak around him, and he saw that he had been stripped of his own clothing and dressed in a tunic of ocher-yellow, and where his limbs showed they had been stained dark. Then they strapped him into his seat again and waited while the copter slowed and dropped toward a landing.

Selden sat rigid, numb with fear and shock, going over and over in his mind the steps by which he had come here and trying to make sense out of them. He could not. One thing was certain, Bentham had deliberately led him into a trap. But why? *Why?* Where were they taking him, what did they mean to do with him? He tried to do positive therapy but it was difficult to remember all the wisdom that had sounded so infinitely wise when he had heard it, and his eyes kept straying to the faces of Altman and Firsa Mak.

There was a quality about them both, something strange that he had never seen before. He tried to analyze what it was. Their flesh appeared to be harder and drier and tougher than normal, their muscles more fibrous and prominent, and there was something about the way they used and carried themselves that reminded him of the large carnivores he had seen in the zoo parks. There was, even more striking, an expression about the eyes and mouth, and Selden realized that these were violent men, men who could strike and tear and perhaps even kill. He was afraid of them. And at the same time he felt superior. He at least was above all that.

The sky had paled. Selden could see desert racing past below. They settled onto it with a great spuming of dust and sand. Atlman and Firsa Mak between them half carried him out of the copter. Their strength was appalling. They moved away from the copter and the backwash of the rotors beat them as it took off. Selden was stricken by the thin air and bitter cold. His bones felt brittle and his lungs were full of knives. The others did not seem to mind. He pulled his cloak tight around him as well as he could with his bound hands, and felt his teeth chattering into the gag. Abruptly Lella reached out and pulled the hood completely down over his face. It had two eyeholes so that it could be used as a mask during sandstorms, but it stifled him and it smelled strangely. He had never felt so utterly miserable.

Dawn was turning the desert to a rusty red. A chain of time-eaten mountains, barren as the fossil vertebrae of some forgotten monster, curved across the northern horizon. Close at hand was a tumbled mass of rocky outcrops, carved to fantastic shapes by wind and sand. From among these rocks there came a caravan.

Selden heard the bells and the padding of broad splayed hooves. The beasts were familiar to him from pictures. Seen in their actual scaly reality, moving across the red sand in that wild daybreak with their burdens and their hooded riders, they were apparitions from some older and uglier time. They came close and stopped, hissing and stamping and rolling their cold bright eyes at Selden, not liking the smell of him in spite of the Martian clothing he wore. They did not seem to mind Altman. Perhaps he had lived with the Martians so long that there was no difference now.

Firsa Mak spoke briefly with the leader of the caravan. The meeting had obviously been arranged, for led animals were brought. The women mounted easily. Selden's stomach turned over at the idea of actually riding one of these creatures. Still, at the moment, he was even more afraid of being left behind, so he made no protest when Firsa Mak and Altman heaved him up onto the saddle pad. One of them rode on each side of him, holding a lead rein. The caravan moved on again, northward toward the mountains.

Within an hour Selden was suffering acutely from cold, thirst, and the unaccustomed exercise. By noon, when they halted to rest, he was almost unconscious. Altman and Firsa Mak helped him down and then carried him around into some rocks where they took the gag out and gave him water. The sun was high now, piercing the thin atmosphere like a burning lance. It scalded Selden's cheeks but at least he was warm, or almost warm. He wanted to stay where he was and die. Altman was quite brutal about it.

"You wanted to go to Jekkara," he said. "Well, you're going . . . just a little bit earlier than you planned, that's all. What the hell, boy, did you think it was all like Kahora?"

And he heaved Selden onto his mount again and they went on.

In midafternoon the wind got up. It never really seemed to stop blowing, but in a tired sort of way, wandering across the sand, picking up a bit of dust and dropping it again, chafing the upthrust rocks a little deeper, stroking the ripple

patterns into a different design. Now it seemed impatient
with everything it had done and determined to wipe it out
and start fresh. It gathered itself and rushed screaming across
the land, and it seemed to Selden that the whole desert
took up and went flying in a red and strangling cloud. The
sun went out. He lost sight of Altman and Firsa Mak at
either end of his reins. He hung in abject terror to his
saddle pad, watching for the small segment of rein he
could see to go slack, when he would know that he was
irretrievably lost. Then as abruptly as it had risen the wind
dropped and the sand resumed its quiet, eternal rolling.

A little while after that, in the long red light from the
west, they dipped down to a line of dark water strung
glittering through the desolation, banded with strips of green
along its sides. There was a smell of wetness and growing
things, and an ancient bridge, and beyond the canal was
a city, with the barren hills behind it.

Selden knew that he was looking at Jekkara. And he was
struck with awe. Even at this late day few Earthmen had
seen it. He stared through the eyeholes of his hood, seeing
at first only the larger masses of rose-red rock, and then
as the sun sank lower and the shadows shifted, making out
the individual shapes of buildings that melted more and more
gently into the parent rock the higher they were on the
sloping cliffs. At one place he saw the ruins of a great
walled castle that he knew had once housed those self-same
Khalide Kings and lord knew how many dynasties before
them in the days when this desert was the bottom of a
blue sea, and there was a lighthouse still standing above
the basin of a dry harbor halfway up the cliffs. He shivered,
feeling the enormous weight of a history in which he and his
had had no part whatever, and it came to him that he had
perhaps been just the tiniest bit presumptuous in his desire
to teach these people.

That feeling lasted him halfway across the bridge. By
that time the western light had gone and the torches were
flaring in the streets of Jekkara, shaken by the dry wind
from the desert. His focus of interest shifted from the then to
the now, and once more he shivered, but for a different
reason. The upper town was dead. The lower town was
not, and there was a quality to the sight and sound and

smell of it that petrified him. Because it was exactly as the early adventurers in their dubious memoirs had described it.

The caravan reached the broad square that fronted the canal, the beasts picking their way protestingly over the sunken, tilted paving stones. People came to meet them. Without his noticing it, Altman and Firsa Mak had maneuvered Selden to the end of the line, and now he found himself being detached and quietly led away up a narrow street between low stone buildings with deep doorways and small window-places, all their corners worn round and smooth as stream-bed rocks by time and the rubbing of countless hands and shoulders. There was something going on in the town, he thought, because he could hear the voices of many people from somewhere beyond, as though they were gathering in a central place. The air smelled of cold and dust, and unfamiliar spices, and less identifiable things.

Altman and Firsa Mak lifted Selden down and held him until his legs regained some feeling. Firsa Mak kept glancing at the sky. Altman leaned close to Selden and whispered, "Do exactly as we tell you, or you won't last the night."

"Nor will we," muttered Firsa Mak, and he tested Selden's gag and made sure his cowl was pulled down to hide his face. "It's almost time."

They led Selden quickly along another winding street. This one was busy and populous. There were sounds and sweet pungent odors and strange-colored lights, and there were glimpses into wickedness of such fantastic array and imaginative genius that Selden's eyes bulged behind his cowl and he remembered his Seminars in Martian Culture with a species of hysteria. Then they came out into a broad square.

It was full of people, cloaked against the night wind and standing quietly, their dark faces still in the shaking light of the torches. They seemed to be watching the sky. Altman and Firsa Mak, with Selden held firmly between them, melted into the edges of the crowd. They waited. From time to time more people came from the surrounding streets, making no sound except for the soft slurring of sandaled feet and the faint elfin chiming of tiny bells beneath the cloaks of the women. Selden found himself watching the sky, though he did not understand why. The crowd seemed to grow more silent, to hold all breath and stirring, and then suddenly over the eastern roofs came the swift moon Denderon, low and red.

The crowd said, "Ah-h-h," a long musical cry of pure despair that shook Selden's heart, and in the same moment harpers who had been concealed in the shadow of a time-worn portico struck their double-banked harps and the cry became a chant, half a lament and half a proud statement of undying hate. The crowd began to move, with the harpers leading and other men carrying torches to light the way. And Selden went with them, up into the hills behind Jekkara.

It was a long cold way under the fleeting light of Denderon. Selden felt the dust of millennia grate and crunch beneath his sandals and the ghosts of cities passed him to the right and left, ruined walls and empty marketplaces and the broken quays where the ships of the Sea-Kings docked. The wild fierce music of the harps sustained and finally dazed him. The long chanting line of people strung out, moving steadily, and there was something odd about the measured rhythm of their pace. It was like a march to the gallows.

The remnants of the works of man were left behind. The barren hills bulked against the stars, splashed with the feeble moonlight that now seemed to Selden to be inexpressibly evil. He wondered why he was no longer frightened. He thought perhaps he had reached the point of complete emotional exhaustion. At any rate he saw things clearly but with no personal involvement.

Even when he saw that the harpers and the torch-bearers were passing into the mouth of a cavern he was not afraid.

The cavern was broad enough for the people to continue marching ten abreast. The harps were muffled now and the chanting took on a deep and hollow tone. Selden felt that he was going downward. A strange and rather terrible eagerness began to stir in him, and this he could not explain at all. The marchers seemed to feel it too, for the pace quickened just a little to the underlying of the harpstrings. And suddenly the rock walls vanished out of sight and they were in a vast cold space that was completely black beyond the pinprick glaring of the torches.

The chanting ceased. The people filed on both sides into a semicircle and stood still, with the harpers at the center and a little group of people in front of them, somehow alone and separate.

One of these people took off the concealing cloak and Selden saw that it was a woman dressed all in purple. For some obscure reason he was sure it was Lella, though the woman's face in the torchlight showed only the smooth gleaming of a silver mask, a very ancient thing with a subtle look of cruel compassion. She took in her hands a pale globed lamp and raised it, and the harpers struck their strings once. The other persons, six in number, laid aside their cloaks. They were three men and three women, all naked and smiling, and now the harps began a tune that was almost merry and the woman in purple swayed her body in time to it. The naked people began to dance, their eyes blank and joyous with some powerful drug, and she led them dancing into the darkness, and as she led them she sang, a long sweet fluting call.

The harps fell silent. Only the woman's voice sounded, and her lamp shone like a dim star, far away.

Beyond the lamp, an eye opened and looked and was aware.

Selden saw the people, the priestess and the six dancing ones, limned momentarily against that orb as seven people might be limned against a risen moon. Then something in him gave way and he fell, clutching oblivion to him like a saving armor.

They spent the remainder of that night and the following day in Firsa Mak's house by the dark canal, and there were sounds of terrible revelry in the streets. Selden sat staring straight ahead, his body shaken by small periodic tremors.

"It isn't true," he said, again and again. "It isn't true."

"It may not be true," Altman said, "but it's a fact. And it's the facts that kill you. Do you understand now why we brought you?"

"You want me to tell the Bureau about . . . about *that.*"

"The Bureau and anyone that will listen."

"But why me? Why not somebody really important, like one of the diplomats?"

"We tried that. Remember Loughlin Herbert?"

"But he died of a heart . . . Oh."

"When Bentham told us about you," Firsa Mak said, "you seemed young and strong enough to stand the shock. We've done all we can now, Selden. For years Altman and I have been trying . . ."

"They won't listen to us," Altman said. "They will not listen. And if they keep sending people in, nice well-meaning children and their meddling nannies, not knowing . . . I simply will not be responsible for the consequences." He looked down at Selden from his gaunt and weathered height.

Firsa Mak said softly, "This is a burden. We have borne it, Selden. We even take pride in bearing it." He nodded toward the unseen hills. "*That* has the power of destruction. Jekkara certainly, and Valkis probably, and Barrakesh, and all the people who depend on this canal for their existence. It can destroy. We know. This is a Martian affair and most of us do not wish to have outsiders brought into it. But Altman is my brother and I must have some care for his people, and I tell you that the Priestess prefers to choose her offerings from among strangers. . . ."

Selden whispered, "How often?"

"Twice a year, when the Mad Moon rises. In between, it sleeps."

"It sleeps," said Altman. "But if it should be roused, and frightened, or made angry . . . For God's sake, Selden, tell them, so that at least they'll *know* what they're getting into."

Selden said wildly, "How can you live here, with that . . ."

Firsa Mak looked at him, surprised that he should ask. "Why," he said, "because we always have."

Selden stared, and thought, and did not sleep, and once he screamed when Lella came softly into the room.

On the second night they slipped out of Jekkara and went back across the desert to the place of rocks, where the copter was waiting. Only Altman returned with Selden. They sat silently in the cabin, and Selden thought, and from time to time he saw Altman watching him, and already in his eyes there was the understanding of defeat.

The glowing domes of Kahora swam out of the dusk, and Denderon was in the sky.

"You're not going to tell them," Altman said.

119

"I don't know," whispered Selden. "I don't know."

Altman left him at the landing stage. Selden did not see him again. He took a cab to his hotel and went directly to his room and locked himself in.

The familiar, normal surroundings aided a return to sanity. He was able to marshal his thoughts more calmly.

If he believed that what he had seen was real, he would have to tell about it, even if no one would listen to him. Even if his superiors, his teachers, his sponsors, the men he venerated and whose approval he yearned for, should be shocked, and look at him with scorn, and shake their heads, and forever close their doors to him. Even if he should be condemned to the outer darkness inhabited by people like Altman and Firsa Mak. Even if.

But if he did not believe that it was real, if he believed instead that it was illusion, hallucination induced by drugs and heaven knew what antique Martian chicanery . . . He had been drugged, that was certain. And Lella *had* practiced some sort of hypnotic technique upon him. . . .

If he did *not* believe . . .

Oh God, how wonderful not to believe, to be free again, to be secure in the body of truth!

He thought, in the quiet and comforting confines of his room, and the longer he thought the more positive his thinking became, the more free of subjectivity, the deeper and calmer in understanding. By the morning he was wan and haggard but healed.

He went to the Bureau and told them that he had been taken ill immediately upon landing, which was why he had not reported. He also told them that he had had urgent word from home and would have to return there at once. They were very sorry to lose him, but most sympathetic, and they booked him onto the first available flight.

A few scars remained on Selden's psyche. He could not bear the sound of a harp nor the sight of a woman wearing purple. These phobias he could have put up with, but the nightmares were just too much. Back on Earth, he went at once to his analyst. He was quite honest with him, and the analyst was able to show him exactly what had happened. The whole affair had been a sex fantasy induced by drugs, with the Priestess a mother-image. The Eye which had looked at him then and which still peered unwinking out of his recurring dreams was symbolic of the female generative principle, and the feeling of horror it aroused in him was due to the guilt complex he had because he was a latent homosexual. Selden was enormously comforted.

The analyst assured him that now that things were healthily out in the open, the secondary effects would fade away. And they might have done so except for the letter.

It arrived just six Martian months after his unfortunate dinner date with Bentham. It was not signed. It said, *"Lella waits for you at moonrise."* And it bore the sketch, very accurately and quite unmistakably done, of a single monstrous eye.

2038: THE ROAD TO SINHARAT

THE DOOR was low, deep-sunk into the thickness of the wall. Carey knocked and then he waited, stooped a bit under the lintelstone, fitting his body to the meager shadow as though he could really hide it there. A few yards away, beyond cracked and tilted paving-blocks, the Jekkara Low Canal showed its still black water to the still black sky, and both were full of stars.

Nothing moved along the canal site. The town was closed tight, and this in itself was so unnatural that it made Carey shiver. He had been here before and he knew how it ought to be. The chief industry of the Low Canal towns is sinning of one sort or another, and they work at it right around the clock. One might have thought that all the people had gone away, but Carey knew they hadn't. He knew that he had not taken a single step unwatched. He had not really believed that they would let him come this far, and he wondered why they had not killed him. Perhaps they remembered him.

There was a sound on the other side of the door.

Carey said in the antique High Martian, "Here is one who claims the guest-right." In Low Martian, the vernacular that fitted more easily on his tongue, he said, "Let me in, Derech. You owe me blood."

The door opened narrowly and Carey slid through it, into lamplight and relative warmth. Derech closed the door and barred it, saying, "Damn you, Carey. I knew you were going to turn up here babbling about blood-debts. I swore I wouldn't let you in."

He was a Low Canaller, lean and small and dark and predatory. He wore a red jewel in his left earlobe and a totally incongruous but comfortable suit of Terran synthetics, insulated against heat and cold. Carey smiled.

"Sixteen years ago," he said, "you'd have perished before you'd have worn that."

"Corruption. Nothing corrupts like comfort, unless it's kindness." Derech sighed. "I knew it was a mistake to let you save my neck that time. Sooner or later you'd claim payment. Well, now that I have let you in, you might as well sit down." He poured wine into a cup of alabaster worn thin as an eggshell and handed it to Carey. They drank, somberly, in silence. The flickering lamplight showed the shadows and the deep lines in Carey's face.

Derech said, "How long since you've slept?"

"I can sleep on the way," said Carey, and Derech looked at him with amber eyes as coldly speculative as a cat's.

Carey did not press him. The room was large, richly furnished with the bare, spare, faded richness of a world that had very little left to give in the way of luxury. Some of the things were fairly new, made in the traditional manner by Martian craftsmen. They were almost indistinguishable from the things that had been old when the Reed Kings and the Bee Kings were little boys along the Nile-bank.

"What will happen," Derech asked, "if they catch you?"

"Oh," said Carey, "they'll deport me first. Then the United Worlds Court will try me, and they can't do anything but find me guilty. They'll hand me over to Earth for punishment, and there will be further investigations and penalties and fines and I'll be a thoroughly broken man when they've finished, and sorry enough for it. Though I think they'll be sorrier in the long run."

"That won't help matters any," said Derech.

"No."

"Why," asked Derech, "why is it that they will not listen?"

"Because they know that they are right."

Derech said an evil word.

"But they do. I've sabotaged the Rehabilitation Project as much as I possibly could. I've rechanneled funds and misdirected orders so they're almost two years behind schedule. These are the things they'll try me for. But my real crime

124

is that I have questioned Goodness and the works thereof. Murder they might forgive me, but not that."

He added wearily, "You'll have to decide quickly. The UW boys are working closely with the Council of City-States, and Jekkara is no longer untouchable. It's also the first place they'll look for me."

"I wondered if that had occurred to you." Derech frowned. "That doesn't bother me. What does bother me is that I know where you want to go. We tried it once, remember? We ran for our lives across that damned desert. Four solid days and nights." He shivered.

"Send me as far as Barrakesh. I can disappear there, join a southbound caravan. I intend to go alone."

"If you intend to kill yourself, why not do it here in comfort and among friends? Let me think," Derech said. "Let me count my years and my treasure and weigh them against a probable yard of sand."

Flames hissed softly around the coals in the brazier. Outside, the wind got up and started its ancient work, rubbing the house walls with tiny grains of dust, rounding off the corners, hollowing the window-places. All over Mars the wind did this, to huts and palaces, to mountains and the small burrow-heaps of animals, laboring patiently toward a day when the whole face of the planet should be one smooth level sea of dust. Only lately new structures of metal and plastic had appeared beside some of the old stone cities. They resisted the wearing sand. They seemed prepared to stay forever. And Carey fancied that he could hear the old wind laughing as it went.

There was a scratching against the closed shutter in the back wall, followed by a rapid drumming of fingertips. Derech rose, his face suddenly alert. He rapped twice on the shutter to say that he understood and then turned to Carey. "Finish your wine."

He took the cup and went into another room with it. Carey stood up. Mingling with the sound of the wind outside, the gentle throb of motors became audible, low in the sky and very near.

Derech returned and gave Carey a shove toward an inner wall. Carey remembered the pivoted stone that was there, and the space behind it. He crawled through the opening.

"Don't sneeze or thrash about," said Derech. "The stone-work is loose, and they'd hear you."

He swung the stone shut. Carey huddled as comfortably as possible in the uneven hole, worn smooth with the hiding of illegal things for countless generations. Air and a few faint gleams of light seeped through between the stone blocks, which were set without mortar as in most Martian construction. He could even see a thin vertical segment of the room.

When the sharp knock came at the door, he discovered that he could hear quite clearly.

Derech moved across his field of vision. The door opened. A man's voice demanded entrance in the name of the United Worlds and the Council of Martian City-States.

"Please enter," said Derech.

Carey saw, more or less fragmentarily, four men. Three were Martians in the undistinguished cosmopolitan garb of the City-States. They were the equivalent of the FBI. The fourth was an Earthman, and Carey smiled to see the measure of his own importance. The spare, blond, good-looking man with the sunburn and the friendly blue eyes might have been an actor, a tennis player, or a junior executive on holiday. He was Howard Wales, Earth's best man in Interpol.

Wales let the Martians do the talking, and while they did it he drifted unobtrusively about, peering through doorways, listening, touching, *feeling*. Carey became fascinated by him, in an unpleasant sort of way. Once he came and stood directly in front of Carey's crevice in the wall. Carey was afraid to breathe, and he had a dreadful notion that Wales would suddenly turn about and look straight in at him through the crack.

The senior Martian, a middle-aged man with an able look about him, was giving Derech a briefing on the penalties that awaited him if he harbored a fugitive or withheld information. Carey thought that he was being too heavy about it. Even five years ago he would not have dared to show his face in Jekkara.

He could picture Derech listening amiably, lounging against something and playing with the jewel in his ear. Finally Derech got bored with it and said without heat, "Because of our geographical position, we have been exposed to the

126

New Culture." The capitals were his. "We have made adjustments to it. But this is still Jekkara and you're here on sufferance, no more. Please don't forget it."

Wales spoke, deftly forestalling any comment from the City-Stater. "You've been Carey's friend for many years, haven't you?"

"We robbed tombs together in the old days."

" 'Archaeological research' is a nicer term, I should think."

"My very ancient and perfectly honorable guild never used it. But I'm an honest trader now, and Carey doesn't come here."

He might have added a qualifying "often," but he did not.

The City-Stater said derisively, "He has or will come here now."

"Why?" asked Derech.

"He needs help. Where else could he go for it?"

"Anywhere. He has many friends. And he knows Mars better than most Martians, probably a damn sight better than you do."

"But," said Wales quietly, "outside of the City-states all Earthmen are being hunted down like rabbits, if they're foolish enough to stay. For Carey's sake, if you know where he is, tell us. Otherwise he is almost certain to die."

"He's a grown man," Derech said. "He must carry his own load."

"He's carrying too much . . ." Wales said, and then broke off. There was a sudden gabble of talk, both in the room and outside. Everybody moved toward the door, out of Carey's vision, except Derech, who moved into it, relaxed and languid and infuriatingly self-assured. Carey could not hear the sound that had drawn the others but he judged that another flier was landing. In a few minutes Wales and the others came back, and now there were some new people with them. Carey squirmed and craned, getting closer to the crack, and he saw Alan Woodthorpe, his superior, Administrator of the Rehabilitation Project for Mars, and probably the most influential man on the planet. Carey knew that he must have rushed across a thousand miles of desert from his headquarters at Kahora, just to be here at this moment.

127

Carey was flattered and deeply moved.

Woodthorpe introduced himself to Derech. He was disarmingly simple and friendly in his approach, a man driven and wearied by many vital matters but never forgetting to be warm, gracious, and human. And the devil of it was that he was exactly what he appeared to be. That was what made dealing with him so impossibly difficult.

Derech said, smiling a little, "Don't stray away from your guards."

"Why is it?" Woodthorpe asked. "Why this hostility? If only your people would understand that we're trying to help them."

"They understand that perfectly," Derech said. "What they can't understand is why, when they have thanked you politely and explained that they neither need nor want your help, you still refuse to leave them alone."

"Because we know what we can do for them! They're destitute now. We can make them rich, in water, in arable land, in power—we can change their whole way of life. Primitive people are notoriously resistant to change, but in time they'll realize . . ."

"Primitive?" said Derech.

"Oh, not the Low Canallers," said Woodthorpe quickly. "Your civilization was flourishing, I know, when Proconsul was still wondering whether or not to climb down out of his tree. For that very reason I cannot understand why you side with the Drylanders."

Derech said, "Mars is an old, cranky, dried-up world, but we understand her. We've made a bargain with her. We don't ask too much of her, and she gives us sufficient for our needs. We can depend on her. We do not want to be made dependent on other men."

"But this is a new age," said Woodthorpe. "Advanced technology makes anything possible. The old prejudices, the parochial viewpoints, are no longer . . ."

"You were saying something about primitives."

"I was thinking of the Dryland tribes. We had counted on Dr. Carey, because of his unique knowledge, to help them understand us. Instead, he seems bent on stirring them up to war. Our survey parties have been set upon with the most shocking violence. If Carey succeeds in reaching the

Drylands there's no telling what he may do. Surely you don't want . . ."

"Primitive," Derech said, with a ring of cruel impatience in his voice. "Parochial. The gods send me a wicked man before a well-meaning fool. Mr. Woodthorpe, the Drylanders do not need Dr. Carey to stir them up to war. Neither do we. We do not want our wells and our water courses re-arranged. We do not want our population expanded. We do not want the resources that will last us for thousands of years yet, if they're not tampered with, pumped out and used up in a few centuries. We are in balance with our environment; we want to stay that way. And we will fight, Mr. Woodthorpe. You're not dealing with theories now. You're dealing with our lives. We are not going to place them in your hands."

He turned to Wales and the Martians. "Search the house. If you want to search the town, that's up to you. But I wouldn't be too long about any of it."

Looking pained and hurt, Woodthorpe stood for a moment and then went out, shaking his head. The Martians began to go through the house. Carey heard Derech's voice say, "Why don't you join them, Mr. Wales?"

Wales answered pleasantly, "I don't like wasting my time." He bade Derech good night and left, and Carey was thankful.

After a while the Martians left too. Derech bolted the door and sat down again to drink his interrupted glass of wine. He made no move to let Carey out, and Carey conquered a very strong desire to yell at him. He was getting just a touch claustrophobic now. Derech sipped his wine slowly, emptied the cup and filled it again. When it was half empty for the second time a girl came in from the back.

She wore the traditional dress of the Low Canals, which Carey was glad to see because some of the women were changing it for the cosmopolitan and featureless styles that made all women look alike, and he thought the old style was charming. Her skirt was a length of heavy orange silk caught at the waist with a broad girdle. Above that she wore nothing but a necklace and her body was slim and graceful as a bending reed. Twisted around her ankles and braided in her dark hair were strings of tiny bells, so that she chimed as she walked with a faint elfin music, very sweet and wicked.

"They're all gone now," she told Derech, and Derech rose and came quickly toward Carey's hiding place.

"Someone was watching through the chinks in the shutters," he said as he helped Carey out. "Hoping I'd betray myself when I thought they were gone." He asked the girl, "It wasn't the Earthman, was it?"

"No." She had poured herself some wine and curled up with it in the silks and warm furs that covered the guest-bench on the west wall. Carey saw that her eyes were green as emerald, slightly tilted, bright, curious and without mercy. He became suddenly very conscious of his unshaven chin and the gray that was beginning to be noticeable at his temples, and his general soiled and weary condition.

"I don't like that man Wales," Derech was saying. "He's almost as good as I am. We'll have him to reckon with yet."

"We," said Carey. "You've weighed your yard of sand?"

Derech shrugged ruefully. "You must have heard me talking myself into it. Well, I've been getting a little bored with the peaceful life." He smiled, the smile Carey remembered from the times they had gone robbing tombs together in places where murder would have been a safer occupation. "And it's always irked me that we were stopped that time. I'd like to try again. By the way, this is Arrin. She'll be going with us as far as Barrakesh."

"Oh." Carey bowed, and she smiled at him from her nest in the soft furs. Then she looked at Derech. "What is there beyond Barrakesh?"

"Kesh," said Derech. "And Shun."

"But you don't trade in the Drylands," she said impatiently. "And if you did, why should I be left behind?"

"We're going to Sinharat," Derech said. "The Ever-living."

"Sinharat?" Arrin whispered. There was a long silence, and then she turned her gaze on Carey. "If I had known that, I would have told them where you were. I would have let them take you." She shivered and bent her head.

"That would have been foolish," Derech said, fondling her. "You'd have thrown away your chance to be the lady of one of the two saviors of Mars."

"If you live," she said.

"But my dear child," said Derech, "can you, sitting there, guarantee to me that you will be alive tomorrow?"

"You will have to admit," said Carey slowly, "that her odds are somewhat better than ours."

II

THE BARGE was long and narrow, buoyed on pontoon-like floats so that it rode high even with a full cargo. Pontoons, hull, and deck were metal. There had not been any trees for shipbuilding for a very long time. In the center of the deck was a low cabin where several people might sleep, and forward toward the blunt bow was a fire-pit where the cooking was done. The motive power was animal, four of the scaly-hided, bad-tempered, hissing beasts of Martian burden plodding along the canal bank with a tow cable.

The pace was slow. Carey had wanted to go across country direct to Barrakesh, but Derech had forbidden it.

"I can't take a caravan. All my business goes by the canal, and everyone knows it. So you and I would have to go alone, riding by night and hiding by day, and saving no time at all." He jabbed his thumb at the sky. "Wales will come when you least expect him and least want him. On the barge you'll have a place to hide, and I'll have enough men to discourage him if he should be rash enough to interfere with a trader going about his normal and lawful business."

"He wouldn't be above it," Carey said gloomily.

"But only when he's desperate. That will be later."

So the barge went gliding gently on its way southward along the thread of dark water that was the last open artery of what had once been an ocean. It ran snow-water now, melted from the polar cap. There were villages beside the canal, and areas of cultivation where long fields showed a startling green against the reddish-yellow desolation. Again there were places where the sand had moved like an army, overwhelming the fields and occupying the houses, so that only mounded heaps would show where a village had been. There were bridges, some of them sound and serving the

131

living, others springing out of nowhere and standing like broken rainbows against the sky. By day there was the stinging sunlight that hid nothing, and by night the two moons laid a shifting loveliness on the land. And if Carey had not been goaded by a terrible impatience he would have been happy.

But all this, if Woodthorpe and the Rehabilitation Project had their way, would go. The waters of the canals would be impounded behind great dams far to the north, and the sparse populations would be moved and settled on new land. Deep-pumping operations, tapping the underground sources that fed the wells, would make up the winter deficit when the cap was frozen. The desert would be transformed, for a space anyway, into a flowering garden. Who would not prefer it to this bitter marginal existence? Who could deny that this was Bad and the Rehabilitation Project Good? No one but the people and Dr. Matthew Carey. And no one would listen to them.

At Sinharat lay the only possible hope of making them listen.

The sky remained empty. Arrin spent most of her time on deck, sitting among the heaped-up bales. Carey knew that she watched him a great deal but he was not flattered. He thought that she hated him because he was putting Derech in danger of his life. He wished that Derech had left her behind.

On the fourth day at dawn the wind dropped to a flat calm. The sun burned hot, setting sand and rock to shimmering. The water of the canal showed a surface like polished glass, and in the east the sharp line of the horizon thickened and blurred and was lost in a yellow haze. Derech stood sniffing like a hound at the still air, and around noon he gave the order to tie up. The crew, ten of them, ceased to lounge on the bales and got to work, driving steel anchor pins for the cables, rigging a shelter for the beasts, checking the lashings of the deck cargo. Carey and Derech worked beside them, and when he looked up briefly from his labors Carey saw Arrin crouched over the fire-pit cooking furiously. The eastern sky became a wall, a wave curling toward the zenith, sooty ocher below, a blazing brass-color at its crest. It rushed across the land, roared, and broke upon them.

They helped each other to the cabin and crouched knee to knee in the tight space, the twelve men and Arrin, while the barge kicked and rolled, sank down deep and shot upward, struggling like a live thing under the blows of the wind. Dust and sand sifted through every vent-hole, tainting the air with a bitter taste. There was a sulfurous darkness, and the ear was deafened. Carey had been through sandstorms before, and he wished that he was out in the open where he was used to it, and where he did not have to worry about the barge turning turtle and drowning him idiotically on the driest world in the System. And while all this was going on, Arrin was grimly guarding her pot.

The wind stopped its wild gusting and settled to a steady gale. When it appeared that the barge was going to remain upright after all, the men ate from Arrin's pot and were glad of the food. After that most of them went down into the hold to sleep because there was more room there.

Arrin put the lid back on the pot and weighted it to keep the sand out, and then she said quietly to Derech, "Why is it that you have to go—where you're going?"

"Because Dr. Carey believes that there are records there that may convince the Rehabilitation people that our 'primitives' know what they are talking about."

Carey could not see her face clearly in the gloom, but he thought she was frowning, thinking hard.

"You believe," she said to Carey. "Do you know?"

"I know that there were records, once. They're referred to in other records. Whether they still exist or not is another matter. But because of the peculiar nature of the place, and of the people who made them, I think it is possible."

He could feel her shiver. "But the Ramas were so long ago."

She barely whispered the name. It meant Immortal, and it had been a word of terror for so long that no amount of time could erase the memory. The Ramas had achieved their immortality by a system of induction that might have been liked to the pouring of old wine into new bottles, and though the principle behind the transplanting of a consciousness from one host to another was purely scientific, the reactions of the people from among whom they requisitioned their supply of hosts was one of simple emotional horror. The Ramas were regarded as vampires. Their ancient island city of Sinharat lay far and forgotten now in the remotest desolation of Shun, and the Drylanders held it holy, and forbidden. They had broken their own taboo just once, when Kynon of Shun raised his banner, claiming to have rediscovered the lost secret of the Ramas and promising the tribesmen and the Low Canallers both eternal life and all the plunder they could carry. He had given them only death and since then the taboo was more fanatically enforced than ever.

"Their city has not been looted," Carey said. "That is why I have hope."

"But," said Arrin, "they weren't human. They were only evil."

"On the contrary. They were completely human. And at one time they made a very great effort to atone."

She turned again to Derech. "The Shunni will kill you."

"That is perfectly possible."

"But you must go." She added shrewdly, "If only to see whether you can."

Derech laughed. "Yes."

"Then I'll go with you. I'd rather see what happens to you than wait and wait and never know." As though that settled it, she curled up in her bunk and went to sleep.

Carey slept too, uneasily, dreaming shadowed dreams of Sinharat and waking from them in the dusty claustrophobic dark to feel hopelessly that he would never see it.

By mid-morning the storm had blown itself out, but now there was a sandbar forty feet long blocking the channel. The beasts were hitched to scoops brought up from the hold and put to dredging, and every man aboard stripped and went in with a shovel.

Carey dug in the wet sand, his taller stature and lighter skin perfectly separating him from the smaller, darker Low Canallers. He felt obvious and naked, and he kept a wary eye cocked toward the heavens. Once he got among the Drylanders, Wales would have to look very hard indeed to spot him. At Valkis, where there was some trade with the desert men, Derech would be able to get him the proper clothing and Carey would arrive at the Gateway, Barrakesh, already in the guise of a wandering tribesman. Until then he would have to be careful, both of Wales and the local canal-dwellers, who had very little to choose between Earthmen and the Drylanders who occasionally raided this far north, stripping their fields and stealing their women.

In spite of Carey's watchfulness, it was Derech who gave the alarm. About the middle of the afternoon he suddenly shouted Carey's name. Carey, laboring now in a haze of sweat and weariness, looked up and saw Derech pointing at the sky. Carey dropped his shovel and dived for the water.

The barge was close by, but the flier came so fast that by the time he had reached the ladder he knew he could not possibly climb aboard without being seen.

Arrin's voice said calmly from overhead, "Dive under. There's room."

Carey caught a breath and dived. The water was cold, and the sunlight slanting through it showed it thick and roiled from the storm. The shadow of the barge made a total darkness into which Carey plunged. When he thought he was clear of the broad pontoons he surfaced, hoping Arrin had told the truth. She had. There was space to breathe, and between the pontoons he could watch the flier come in low and hover on its rotors above the canal, watching. Then it landed. There were several men in it, but only Howard Wales got out.

Derech went to talk to him. The rest of the men kept on working, and Carey saw that the extra shovel had vanished into the water. Wales kept looking at the barge. Derech was playing with him, and Carey cursed. The icy chill of the water was biting him to the bone. Finally, to Wales' evident surprise, Derech invited him aboard. Carey swam carefully back and forth in the dark space under the hull, trying to keep his blood moving. After a long long time, a year or two, he saw Wales walking back to the flier. It seemed another year before the flier took off. Carey fought his way out from under the barge and into the sunlight again, but he was too stiff and numb to climb the ladder. Arrin and Derech had to pull him up.

"Anyone else," said Derech, "would be convinced. But

this one—he gives his opponent credit for all the brains and deceitfulness he needs."

He poured liquor between Carey's chattering teeth and wrapped him in thick blankets and put him in a bunk. Then he said, "Could Wales have any way of guessing where we're going?"

Carey frowned. "I suppose he could, if he bothered to go through all my monographs and papers."

"I'm sure he's bothered."

"It's all there," Carey said dismally. "How we tried it once and failed—and what I hoped to find, though the Rehabilitation Act hadn't come along then, and it was pure archaeological interest. And I have, I know, mentioned the Ramas to Woodthorpe when I was arguing with him about the advisability of all these earth-shattering—mars-shattering—changes. Why? Did Wales say something?"

"He said, 'Barrakesh will tell the story.' "

"He did, did he?" said Carey viciously. "Give me the bottle." He took a long pull and the liquor went into him like fire into glacial ice. "I wish to heaven I'd been able to steal a flier."

Derech shook his head. "You're lucky you didn't. They'd have had you out of the sky in an hour."

"Of course you're right. It's just that I'm in a hurry." He drank again and then he smiled, a very unscholarly smile. "If the gods are good to me, someday I'll have Mr. Wales between my hands."

The local men came along that evening, about a hundred of them with teams and implements. They had already worked all day clearing other blocks, but they worked without question all that night and into the next day, each man choosing his own time to fall out and sleep when he could no longer stand up. The canal was their life, and their law said that the canal came first, before wife, child, brother, parent, or self, and it was a hanging matter. Carey stayed out of sight in the cabin, feeling guilty about not helping but not too guilty. It was backbreaking work. They had the channel clear by the middle of the morning, and the barge moved on southward.

Three days later a line of cliffs appeared in the east, far

away at first but closing gradually until they marched beside the canal. They were high and steep, colored softly in shades of red and gold. The faces of the rock were fantastically eroded by a million years of water and ten millennia of wind. These were the rim of the sea basin, and presently Carey saw in the distance ahead a shimmering line of mist on the desert where another canal cut through it. They were approaching Valkis.

It was sunset when they reached it. The low light struck in level shafts against the cliffs. Where the angle was right, it shone through the empty doors and window holes of the five cities that sprawled downward over the ledges of red-gold rock. It seemed as though hearthfires burned there, and warm lamplight to welcome home men weary from the sea. But in the streets and squares and on the long flights of rock-cut steps only slow shadows moved with the sinking sun. The ancient quays stood stark as tombstones, marking the levels where new harbors had been built and then abandoned as the water left them, and the high towers that had flown the banners of the Sea-Kings were bare and broken.

Only the lowest city lived, and only a part of that, but it lived fiercely, defiant of the cold centuries towering over it. From the barge deck Carey watched the torches flare out like yellow stars in the twilight, and he heard voices, and the wild and lovely music of the double-banked harps. The dry wind had a smell in it of dusty spices and strange exotic things. The New Culture had not penetrated here, and Carey was glad, though he did think that Valkis could stand being cleaned up just a little without hurting it any. They had two or three vices for sale there that were quite unbelievable.

"Stay out of sight," Derech told him, "till I get back."

It was full dark when they reached their mooring, at an ancient stone dock beside a broad square with worn old buildings on three sides of it. Derech went into the town and so did the crew, but for different reasons. Arrin stayed on deck, lying on the bales with her chin on her wrists, staring at the lights and listening to the noises like a sulky child forbidden to play some dangerous but fascinating game. Derech did not allow her in the streets alone.

Out of sheer boredom, Carey went to sleep.

He did not know how long he had slept, a few minutes or a few hours, when he was wakened sharply by Arrin's wildcat scream.

III

THERE WERE men on the deck outside. Carey could hear them scrambling around and cursing the woman, and someone was saying something about an Earthman. He rolled out of his bunk. He was still wearing the Earth-made coverall that was all the clothing he had until Derech came back. He stripped it off in a wild panic and shoved it far down under the tumbled furs. Arrin did not scream again but he thought he could hear muffled sounds as though she were trying to. He shivered, naked in the chill dark.

Footsteps came light and swift across the deck. Carey reached out and lifted from its place on the cabin wall a long-handled ax that was used to cut loose the deck cargo lashings in case of emergency. And as though the ax had spoken to him, Carey knew what he was going to do.

The shapes of men appeared in the doorway, dark and huddled against the glow of the deck lights.

Carey gave a Dryland war-cry that split the night. He leaped forward, swinging the ax.

The men disappeared out of the doorway as though they had been jerked on strings. Carey emerged from the cabin onto the deck, where the torchlight showed him clearly, and he whirled the ax around his head as he had learned to do years ago when he first understood both the possibility and the immense value of being able to go Martian. Inevitably he had got himself embroiled in unscholarly, unarchaeological matters like tribal wars and raiding, and he had acquired some odd skills. Now he drove the dark, small, startled men ahead of the ax-blade. Yelling, he drove them in the torchlight while they stared at him, five astonished men with silver rings in their ears and very sharp knives in their belts.

Carey quoted some Dryland sayings about Low Canallers

138

that brought the blood flushing into their cheeks. Then he asked them what their business was.

One of them, who wore a kilt of vivid yellow, said, "We were told there was an Earthman hiding."

And who told you? Carey wondered. Mr. Wales, through some Martian spy? Of course, Mr. Wales—who else? He was beginning to hate Mr. Wales. But he laughed and said, "Do I look like an Earthman?"

He made the ax-blade flicker in the light. He let his hair grow long and ragged, and it was a good desert color, tawny brown. His naked body was lean and long-muscled like a desert man's, and he had kept it hard. Arrin came up to him, rubbing her bruised mouth and staring at him as surprised as the Valkisians.

The man in the yellow kilt said again, "We were told . . ."

Other people had begun to gather in the dockside square, both men and women, idle, curious, and cruel.

"My name is Marah," Carey said. "I left the Wells of Tamboina with a price on my head for murder." The Wells were far enough away that he need not fear a fellow-tribesman rising to dispute his story. "Does anybody here want to collect it?"

The people watched him. The torch flames blew in the dry wind, scattering the light across their upturned faces. Carey began to be afraid.

Close beside him Arrin whispered, "Will you be recognized?"

"No." He had been here three times with Dryland bands but it was hardly likely that anyone would remember one specific tribesman out of the numbers that floated through.

"Then stand steady," Arrin said.

He stood. The people watched him, whispering and smiling among themselves. Then the man in the yellow kilt said, "Earthman or Drylander, I don't like your face."

The crowd laughed, and a forward movement began. Carey could hear the sweet small chiming of the bells the women wore. He gripped the ax and told Arrin to get away from him. "If you know where Derech's gone, go after him. I'll hold them as long as I can."

He did not know whether she left him or not. He was watching the crowd, seeing the sharp blades flash. It seemed

139

ridiculous, in this age of space flight and atomic power, to be fighting with ax and knife. But Mars had had nothing better for a long time, and the UW Peace and Disarmament people hoped to take even those away from them someday. On Earth, Carey remembered, there were still peoples who hardened their wooden spears in the fire and ate their enemies. The knives, in any case, could kill efficiently enough. He stepped back a little from the rail to give the ax free play, and he was not cold any longer, but warm with a heat that stung his nerve-ends.

Derech's voice shouted across the square.

The crowd paused. Carey could see over their heads to where Derech, with about half his crew around him, was forcing his way through. He looked and sounded furious.

"I'll kill the first man that touches him!" he yelled.

The man in the yellow kilt asked politely, "What is he to you?"

"He's money, you fool! Passage money that I won't collect till I reach Barrakesh, and not then unless he's alive and able to get it for me. And if he doesn't, I'll see to him myself." Derech sprang up onto the barge deck. "Now clear off. Or you'll have more killing to do than you'll take pleasure in."

His men were lined up with him now along the rail, and the rest of the crew were coming. Twelve tough armed men did not look like much fun. The crowd began to drift away, and the original five went reluctantly with them. Derech posted a watch and took Carey into the cabin.

"Get into these," he said, throwing down a bundle he had taken from one of the men. Carey laid aside his ax. He was shaking now with relief and his fingers stumbled over the knots. The outer wrapping was a thick desert cloak. Inside was a leather kilt, well worn and adorned with clanking bronze bosses, a wide bronze collar for the neck and a leather harness for weapons that was black with use.

"They came off a dead man," Derech said. "There are sandals underneath." He took a long desert knife from his girdle and tossed it to Carey. "And this. And now, my friend, we are in trouble."

"I thought I did rather well," Carey said, buckling kilt and harness. They felt good. Perhaps someday, if he lived, he

140

would settle down to being the good gray Dr. Carey, archaeologist emeritus, but the day was not yet. "Someone told them there was an Earthman here."

Derech nodded. "I have friends here, men who trust me, men I trust. They warned me. That's why I routed my crew out of the brothels, and unhappy they were about it, too."

Carey laughed. "I'm grateful to them." Arrin had come in and was sitting on the edge of her bunk, watching Carey. He swung the cloak around him and hooked the bronze catch at the throat. The rough warmth of the cloth was welcome. "Wales will know now that I'm with you. This was his way of finding out for sure."

"You might have been killed," Arrin said.

Carey shrugged. "It wouldn't be a calamity. They'd rather have me dead than lose me, though of course none of them would dream of saying so. Point is, he won't be fooled by the masquerade, and he won't wait for Barrakesh. He'll be on board as soon as you're well clear of Valkis and he'll have enough force with him to make it good."

"All true," said Derech. "So. Let him have the barge." He turned to Arrin. "If you're still hell-bent to come with us, get ready. And remember, you'll be riding for a long time."

To Carey he said, "Better keep clear of the town. I'll have mounts and supplies by the time Phobos rises. Where shall we meet?"

"By the lighthouse," Carey said. Derech nodded and went out. Carey went out too and waited on the deck while Arrin changed her clothes. A few minutes later she joined him, wrapped in a long cloak. She had taken the bells from her hair and around her ankles, and she moved quietly now, light and lithe as a boy. She grinned at him. "Come, desert man. What did you say your name was?"

"Marah."

"Don't forget your ax."

They left the barge. Only one torch burned now on the deck. Some of the lights had died around the square. This was deserted, but there was still sound and movement in plenty along the streets that led into it. Carey guided Arrin to the left along the canal bank. He did not see anyone watching them, or following them. The sounds and the lights grew fainter. The buildings they passed now were empty, their doors and windows open to the wind. Deimos was in the sky, and some of the roofs showed moonlight through them, shafts of pale silver touching the drifted dust that covered the floors. Carey stopped several times to listen, but he heard nothing except the wind. He began to feel better. He hurried Arrin with long strides, and now they moved away from the canal and up a broken street that led toward the cliffs.

The street became a flight of steps cut in the rock. There were roofless stone houses on either side, clinging to the cliffs row on ragged row like the abandoned nests of sea-birds. Carey's imagination, as always, peopled them, hung them with nets and gear, livened them with lights and voices and appropriate smells. At the top of the steps he paused to let Arrin get her breath, and he looked down across the centuries at the torches of Valkis burning by the canal.

"What are you thinking?" Arrin asked.

"I'm thinking that nothing, not people nor oceans, should ever die."

"The Ramas lived forever."

"Too long, anyway. And that wasn't good, I know. But still it makes me sad to think of men building these houses and working and raising their families, looking forward to the future."

"You're an odd one," Arrin said. "When I first met you I couldn't understand what it was that made Derech love you. You were so—quiet. Tonight I could see. But now you've gone all broody and soft again. Why do you care so much about dust and old bones?"

"Curiosity. I'll never know the end of the story, but I can at least know the beginning."

They moved on again, and now they were walking across the basin of a harbor, with the great stone quays towering above them, gnawed and rounded by the wind. Ahead on a crumbling promontory the shaft of a broken tower pointed skyward. They came beneath it, where ships had used to come, and presently Carey heard the jingling and padding of animals coming toward them. Before the rise of Phobos they were mounted and on their way.

142

"This is your territory," said Derech. "I will merely ride."

"Then you and Arrin can handle the pack animals." Carey took the lead. They left the city behind, climbing to the top of the cliffs. The canal showed like a ribbon of steel in the moonlight far below, and then was gone. A range of mountains had come down here to the sea, forming a long curving peninsula. Only their bare bones were left, and through that skeletal mass of rock Carey took his little band by a trail he had followed once and hoped that he remembered.

They traveled all that way by night, lying in the shelter of the rocks by day, and three times a flier passed over them like a wheeling hawk, searching. Carey thought more than once that he had lost the way, though he never said so, and he was pleasantly surprised when they found the sea bottom again just where it should be on the other side of the range, with the ford he remembered across the canal. They crossed it by moonlight, stopping only to fill up their water bags. At dawn they were on a ridge above Barrakesh.

They looked down, and Derech said, "I think we can forget about our southbound caravan."

Trade was for times of peace, and now the men of Kesh and Shun were gathering for war, even as Derech had said, without need of any Dr. Carey to stir them to it.

They filled the streets. They filled the *serais*. They camped in masses by the gates and along the banks of the canal and around the swampy lake that was its terminus. The vast herds of animals broke down the dikes, trampled the irrigation ditches and devoured the fields. And across the desert more riders were coming, long files of them with pennons waving and lances glinting in the morning light. Wild and far away, Carey heard the skirling of the desert pipes.

"The minute we go down there," he said, "we are part of the army. Any man that turns his back on Barrakesh now will get a spear through it for cowardice."

His face became hard and cruel with a great rage. Presently this horde would roll northward, sweeping up more men from the Low Canal towns as it passed, joining ultimately with other hordes pouring in through the easterly gates of the Drylands. The people of the City-States would fall like butchered sheep, and perhaps even the dome of Kahora would come shattering down. But sooner or later the guns would be brought up, and then the Drylanders would do the falling, all because of good men like Woodthorpe who only wanted to help.

Carey said, "I am going to Sinharat. But you know how much chance a small party has, away from the caravan track and the wells."

"I know," said Derech.

"You know how much chance we have of evading Wales, without the protection of a caravan."

"You tell me how I can go quietly home, and I'll do it."

"You can wait for your barge and go back to Valkis."

"I couldn't do that," Derech said seriously. "My men would laugh at me. I suggest we stop wasting time. Here in the desert, time is water."

"Speaking of water," Arrin said, "how about when we get there? And how about getting back?"

Derech said, "Dr. Carey has heard that there is a splendid well at Sinharat."

"He's heard," said Arrin, "but he doesn't know. Same as the records." She gave Carey a look, only half scornful.

Carey smiled briefly. "The well I have on pretty good authority. It's in the coral deep under the city, so it can be used without actually breaking the taboo. The Shunni don't go near it unless they're desperate, but I talked to a man who had."

He led them down off the ridge and away from Barrakesh. And Derech cast an uneasy glance at the sky.

"I hope Wales did set a trap for us there. And I hope he'll sit a while waiting for us to spring it."

There was a strict law against the use of fliers over tribal lands without special permission, which would be unprocurable now. But they both knew that Wales would not let that stop him.

"The time could come," Carey said grimly, "that we'd be glad to see him."

He led them a long circle northward to avoid the war parties coming into Barrakesh. Then he struck out across the deadly waste of the sea bottom, straight for Sinharat.

He lost track of time very quickly. The days blurred together into one endless hell wherein they three and the staggering animals toiled across vast slopes of rock up-tilted to the sun, or crept under reefs of rotten coral with sand around them as smooth and bright as a burning-glass. At night there was moonlight and bitter cold, but the cold did nothing to alleviate their thirst. There was only one good thing about the journey, and that was the thing that worried Carey the most. In all that cruel and empty sky, no flier ever appeared.

"The desert is a big place," Arrin said, looking at it with loathing. "Perhaps he couldn't find us. Perhaps he's given up."

"Not him," said Carey.

Derech said, "Maybe he thinks we're dead anyway, and why bother."

Maybe, Carey thought. *Maybe*. But sometimes as he rode or walked he would curse at Wales out loud and glare at the sky, demanding to know what he was up to. There was never any answer.

The last carefully-hoarded drop of water went. And Carey forgot about Wales and thought only of the well of Sinharat, cold and clear in the coral.

He was thinking of it as he plodded along, leading the beast that was now almost as weak as he. The vision of the well so occupied him that it was some little time before the message from his bleared and sun-struck eyes got through it and registered on his brain. Then he halted in sudden wild alarm.

He was walking, not on smooth sand, but in the trampled marks of many riders.

IV

THE OTHERS came out of their stupor as he pointed, warning them to silence. The broad track curved ahead and vanished out of sight beyond a great reef of white coral. The wind had not had time to do more than blur the edges of the individual prints.

Mounting and whipping their beasts unmercifully, Carey and the others fled the track. The reef stood high above them like a wall. Along its base were cavernous holes, and they found one big enough to hold them all. Carey went on alone and on foot to the shoulder of the reef, where the riders had turned it, and the wind went with him, piping and crying in the vast honeycomb of the coral.

He crept around the shoulder and then he saw where he was.

On the other side of the reef was a dry lagoon, stretching perhaps half a mile to a coral island that stood up tall in the hard clear sunlight, its naked cliffs beautifully striated with deep rose and white and delicate pink. A noble stairway went up from the desert to a city of walls and towers so perfectly built from many-shaded marble and so softly sculptured by time that it was difficult to tell where the work of men began and ended. Carey saw it through a shimmering haze of exhaustion and wonder, and knew that he looked at Sinharat, the Ever-Living.

The trampled track of the Shunni warriors went out across the lagoon. It swept furiously around what had been a parked flier, and then passed on, leaving behind it battered wreckage and two dark sprawled shapes. It ended at the foot of the cliffs, where Carey could see a sort of orderly turmoil of men and animals. There were between twenty-five and thirty warriors, as nearly as he could guess. They were making camp.

Carey knew what that meant. There was someone in the city.

Carey did not move for some time. He stared at the beautiful marble city shimmering on its lovely pedestal of coral. He wanted to weep, but there was not enough moisture left in him to make tears, and his despair was gradually replaced by a feeble anger. *All right, you bastards,* he thought. *All right!*

He went back to Derech and Arrin and told them what he had seen.

"Wales just came ahead of us and waited. Why bother to search a whole desert when he knew where we were going? This time he'd have us for sure. Water. We couldn't run away." Carey grinned horribly with his cracked lips and swollen tongue. "Only the Shunni found him first. War party. They must have seen the flier go over—came to check

146

if it landed here. Caught two men in it. But the rest are in Sinharat."

"How do you know?" asked Derech.

"The Shunni won't go into the city except as a last resort. If they catch a trespasser there they just hold the well and wait. Sooner or later he comes down."

Arrin said, "How long can we wait? We've had no water for two days."

"Wait, hell," said Carey. "We can't wait. I'm going in."

Now, while they still had a shred of strength. Another day would be too late.

Derech said, "I suppose a quick spear is easier than thirst."

"We may escape both," said Carey, "if we're very careful. And very lucky."

He told them what to do.

An hour or so later Carey followed the warriors' track out across the dry lagoon. He walked, or rather staggered, leading the animals. Arrin rode on one, her cloak pulled over her head and her face covered in sign of mourning. Between two of the beasts, on an improvised litter made of blankets and pack lashings, Derech lay wrapped from head to foot in his cloak, a too-convincing imitation of a corpse. Carey heard the shouts and saw the distant riders start toward them, and he was frightened. The smallest slip, the most minor mistake, could give them away, and then he did not think that anything on Mars could save them. But thirst was more imperative than fear.

There was something more. Carey passed the two bodies in the sand beside the wrecked flier. He saw that they were both dark-haired Martians, and he looked at the towers of Sinharat with wolfish eyes. Wales was up there, still alive, still between him and what he wanted. Carey's hand tightened on the ax. He was no longer entirely sane on the subject of Howard Wales and the records of the Ramas.

When the riders were within spear range he halted and rested the axhead in the sand, as a token. He waited, saying softly, "For God's sake now, be careful."

The riders reined in, sending the sand flying. Carey said to them, "I claim the death right."

He stood swaying over his ax while they looked at him,

147

and at the muffled woman, and at the dusty corpse. They were six, tall, hard fierce-eyed men with their long spears held ready. Finally one of them said, "How did you come here?"

"My sister's husband," said Carey, indicating Derech, "died on the march to Barrakesh. Our tribal law says he must rest in his own place. But there are no caravans now. We had to come alone, and in a great sandstorm we lost the track. We wandered for many days until we crossed your trail."

"Do you know where you are?" asked the Drylander.

Carey averted his eyes from the city. "I know now. But if a man is dying it is permitted to use the well. We are dying."

"Use it, then," said the Drylander. "But keep your ill omen away from our camp. We are going to the war as soon as we finish our business here. We want no corpse-shadow on us."

"Outlanders?" Carey asked, a rhetorical question in view of the flier and the un-Dryland bodies.

"Outlanders. Who else is foolish enough to wake the ghosts in the Forbidden City?"

Carey shook his head. "Not I. I do not wish even to see it."

The riders left them, returning to the camp. Carey moved on slowly toward the cliffs. It became apparent where the well must be. A great arching cave-mouth showed in the rose-pink coral and men were coming and going there, watering their animals. Carey approached it and began the monotonous chant that etiquette required, asking that way be made for the dead, so that warriors and pregnant women and persons undergoing ritual purifications would be warned to go aside. The warriors made way. Carey passed out of the cruel sunlight into the shadow of an irregular vaulted passage, quite high and wide, with a floor that sloped upward, at first gently and then steeply, until suddenly the passage ended in an echoing cathedral room dim-lit by torches that picked out here and there the shape of a fantastic flying buttress of coral. In the center of the room, in a kind of broad basin, was the well.

Now for the first time Arrin broke her silence with a soft

anguished cry. There were seven or eight warriors guarding the well, as Carey had known there would be, but they drew away and let Carey's party severely alone. Several men were in the act of watering their mounts, and as though in deference to taboo Carey circled around to get as far away from them as possible. In the gloom he made out the foot of an age-worn stairway leading upward through the coral. Here he stopped.

He helped Arrin down and made her sit, and then dragged Derech from the litter and laid him on the hard coral. The animals bolted for the well and he made no effort to hold them. He filled one of the bags for Arrin and then he flung himself alongside the beasts and drank and soaked himself in the beautiful cold clear water. After that he crouched still for a few moments, in a kind of daze, until he remembered that Derech too needed water.

He filled two more bags and took them to Arrin, kneeling beside her as though in tender concern as she sat beside her dead. His spread cloak covered what she was doing, holding the water bag to Derech's mouth so that he could drink. Carey spoke softly and quickly. Then he went back to the animals. He began to fight them away from the water so that they should not founder themselves. The activity covered what was going on in the shadows behind them. Carey led them, hissing and stamping, to where Arrin and Derech had been, still using them as a shield in case the guards were watching. He snatched up his ax and the remaining water bag and let the animals go and ran fast as he could up the stairway. It spiraled, and he was stumbling in pitch-darkness around the second curve before the guards below let out a great angry cry.

He did not know whether they would follow or not. Somebody fumbled for him in the blackness and Derech's voice muttered something urgent. He could hear Arrin panting like a spent hound. His own knees shook with weakness and he thought what a fine militant crew they were to be taking on Wales and his men and thirty angry Shunni. Torchlight flickered against the turn of the wall below and there was a confusion of voices. They fled upward, pulling each other along, and it seemed that the Shunni reached a point beyond which they did not care to go. The torchlight and the voices vanished. Carey and the others climbed a little farther and then dropped exhausted on the worn treads.

Arrin asked, "Why didn't they follow us?"

"Why should they? Our water won't last long. They can wait."

"Yes," said Arrin. And then, "How *are* we going to get away?"

Carey answered, "That depends on Wales."

"I don't understand."

"On whether, and how soon, somebody sends a flier out here to see what happened to him." He patted the water bags. "That's why these are so important. They give us time."

They started up the stair again, treading in the worn hollows made by other feet. The Ramas must have come this way for water for a very long time. Presently a weak daylight filtered down to them. And then a man's voice, tight with panic, cried out somewhere above them, "I hear them! They're coming. . . ."

The voice of Howard Wales answered sharply. "Wait!" Then in English it called down, "Carey. Dr. Carey. Is that you?"

"It is," Carey shouted back.

"Thank Heaven," said Wales. "I saw you, but I wasn't sure. . . . Come up, man, come up, and welcome. We're all in the same trap now."

V

SINHARAT was a city without people, but it was not dead. It had a memory and a voice. The wind gave it breath, and it sang, from the countless tiny organ-pipes of the coral, from the hollow mouths of marble doorways and the narrow throats of streets. The slender towers were like tall flutes, and the wind was never still. Sometimes the voice of Sinharat was soft and gentle, murmuring about everlasting youth and the pleasures thereof. Again it was strong and fierce with pride, crying, *You die, but I do not!* Sometimes it was mad, laughing and hateful. But always the song was evil.

Carey could understand now why Sinharat was taboo. It

was not only because of an ancient dread. It was the city itself, now, in the sharp sunlight or under the gliding moons. It was a small city. There had never been more than perhaps three thousand Ramas, and this remote little island had given them safety and room enough. But they had built close, and high. The streets ran like topless tunnels between the walls and the towers reached impossibly thin and tall into the sky. Some of them had lost their upper stories and some had fallen entirely, but in the main they were still beautiful. The colors of the marble were still lovely. Many of the buildings were perfect and sound, except that wind and time had erased the carvings on their walls so that only in certain angles of light did a shadowy face leap suddenly into being, prideful and mocking with smiling lips, or a procession pass solemnly toward some obliterated worship.

Perhpas it was only the wind and the half-seen watchers that gave Sinharat its feeling of eerie wickedness. Carey did not think so. The Ramas had built something of themselves into their city, and it was rather, he imagined, as one of the Rama women might have been had one met her, graceful and lovely but with something wrong about the eyes. Even the matter-of-fact Howard Wales was uncomfortable in the city, and the three surviving City-State men who were with him went about like dogs with their tails tight to their bellies. Even Derech lost some of his cheerful arrogance, and Arrin never left his side.

The feeling was worse inside the buildings. Here were the halls and chambers where the Ramas had lived. Here were the possessions they had handled, the carvings and faded frescoes they had looked at. The ever-young, the Ever-living immortals, the stealers of others' lives, had walked these corridors and seen themselves reflected in the surfaces of polished marble, and Carey's nerves quivered with the nearness of them after all this long time.

There were traces of a day when Sinharat had had an advanced technology equal to, if not greater, than any Carey had yet seen on Mars. The inevitable reversion to the primitive had come with the exhaustion of resources. There was one rather small room where much wrecked equipment lay in crystal shards and dust, and Carey knew that this was the place where the Ramas had exchanged their old bodies for new. From some of the frescoes, done with brilliantly sadistic humor, he knew that the victims were generally killed soon, but not too soon, after the exchange was completed.

Still he could not find the place where the archives had been kept. Outside, Wales and his men, generally with Derech's help and Arrin as a lookout, were sweating to clear away rubble from the one square that was barely large enough for a flier to land in. Wales had been in contact with Kahora before the unexpected attack. They knew where he was, and when there had been too long a time without a report from him they would certainly come looking. If they had a landing place cleared by then, and the scanty water supply, severely rationed, kept them alive, and the Shunni did not become impatient, they would be all right.

"Only," Carey told them, "if that flier does come, be ready to jump quick. Because the Shunni will attack then."

He had not had any trouble with Howard Wales. He had expected it. He had come up the last of the stairway with his ax ready. Wales shook his head. "I have a heavy-duty shocker," he said. "Even so, I wouldn't care to take you on. You can put down the ax, Dr. Carey."

The Martians were armed too. Carey knew they could have taken him easily. Perhaps they were saving their charges against the Shunni, who played the game of war for keeps.

Carey said, "I will do what I came here to do."

Wales shrugged. "My assignment was to bring you in. I take it there won't be any more trouble about that now—if any of us get out of here. Incidentally, I saw what was happening at Barrakesh, and I can testify that you could not possibly have had any part in it. I'm positive that some of my superiors are thundering asses, but that's nothing new, either. So go ahead. I won't hinder you."

Carey had gone ahead, on a minimum of water, sleep, and the dry desert rations he had in his belt-pouch. Two and a half days were gone, and the taste of defeat was getting stronger in his mouth by the hour. Time was getting short, no one could say how short. And then almost casually he crawled over a great fallen block of marble into a long room with rows of vault doors on either side, and a hot wave of excitement burned away his weariness. The bars of beautiful rustless alloy slid easily under his hands. And he was dazed at the treasure of knowledge that he had found, tortured by the realization that he could only take a fraction of it with him and might well never see the rest of it again.

The Ramas had arranged their massive archives according to a simple and orderly dating system. It did not take him long to find the records he wanted, but even that little time was almost too much.

Derech came shouting after him. Carey closed the vault he was in and scrambled back over the fallen block, clutching the precious spools. "Flier!" Derech kept saying. "Hurry!" Carey could hear the distant cries of the Shunni.

He ran with Derech and the cries came closer. The warriors had seen the flier too and now they knew that they must come into the city. Carey raced through the narrow twisting street that led to the square. When he came into it he could see the flier hanging on its rotors about thirty feet overhead, very ginger about coming down in that cramped space. Wales and the Martians were frantically waving. The Shunni came in two waves, one from the well-stair and one up the cliffs. Carey picked up his ax. The shockers began to crackle.

He hoped they would hold the Drylanders off because he did not want to have to kill anyone, and he particularly did not want to get killed, not right now. "Get to the flier!" Wales yelled at him, and he saw that it was just settling down, making a great wind and dust. The warriors in the forefront of the attack were dropping or staggering as the stunning charges hit them, sparking off their metal ornaments and the tips of their spears. The first charge was broken up, but no one wanted to stay for the second. Derech had Arrin and was lifting her bodily into the flier. Hands reached out and voices shouted unnecessary pleas for haste. Carey threw away his ax and jumped for the hatch. The Martians crowded in on top of him and then Wales, and the pilot took off so abruptly that Wales' legs were left dangling outside. Carey caught him and pulled him in. Wales laughed, in an odd wild way, and the flier rose up among the towers of Sinharat in a rattle of flung spears.

The technicians had had trouble regearing their equipment to the Rama microtapes. The results were still far from perfect, but the United Worlds Planetary Assistance Committee, hastily assembled at Kahora, were not interested in perfection. They were Alan Woodthorpe's superiors, and they had a decision to make, and little time in which to make it. The great tide was beginning to roll north out of the Drylands, moving at the steady marching pace of the desert beasts. And Woodthorpe could no longer blame this all on Carey.

Looking subdued and rather frightened, Woodthorpe sat beside Carey in the chamber where the hearing was being held. Derech was there, and Wales, and some high brass from the City-States who were getting afraid for their borders, and two Dryland chiefs who knew Carey as Carey, not as a tribesman, and trusted him enough to come in. Carey thought bitterly that this hearing should have been held long ago. Only the Committee had not understood the potential seriousness of the situation. They had been told, plainly and often. But they had preferred to believe experts like Woodthorpe rather than men like Carey, who had some specialized knowledge but were not trained to evaluate the undertaking as a whole.

Now in a more chastened mood they watched as Carey's tapes went whispering through the projectors.

They saw an island city in a blue sea. People moved in its streets. There were ships in its harbors and the sounds of life. Only the sea had shrunk down from the tops of the coral cliffs. The lagoon was a shallow lake wide-rimmed with beaches, and the outer reef stood bare above a feeble surf. A man's voice spoke in the ancient High Martian, somewhat distorted by the reproduction and blurred by the voice of a translator speaking Esperanto. Carey shut his ears to everything but the voice, the man, who spoke across the years.

"Nature grins at us these days, reminding us that even planets die. We who have loved life so much that we have taken the lives of countless others in order to retain it, can now see the beginning of our inevitable end. Even though this may yet be thousands of years in the future, the thought of it has had strange effects. For the first time some of our people are voluntarily choosing death. Others demand younger and younger hosts, and change them constantly. Most of us have come to have some feeling of remorse, not for our immortality but for the method by which we achieved it.

"One murder can be remembered and regretted. Ten thousand murders become as meaningless as ten thousand love affairs or ten thousand games of chess. Time and repetition grind them all to the same dust. Yet now we do regret, and a naïve passion has come to us, a passion to be forgiven, if not by our victims then perhaps by ourselves.

"Thus our great project is undertaken. The people of Kharif, because their coasts are accessible and their young people exceptionally handsome and sturdy, have suffered more from us than any other single nation. We will try to make some restitution."

The scene shifted from Sinharat to a desolated stretch of desert coastline beside the shrunken sea. The land had once been populous. There were the remains of cities and towns, connected by paved roads. There had been factories and power stations, all the appurtenances of an advanced technology. These were now rusting away, and the wind blew ocher dust to bury them.

"For a hundred years," said the Rama voice, "it has not rained."

There was an oasis, with wells of good water. Tall brown-haired men and women worked the well-sweeps, irrigating fields of considerable extent. There was a village of neat huts, housing perhaps a thousand people.

"Mother Mars has killed far more of her children than we. The fortunate survivors live in 'cities' like these. The less fortunate . . ."

A long line of beasts and hooded human shapes moved across a bitter wasteland. And the Dryland chiefs cried out, "Our people!"

"We will give them water again," said the Rama voice.

The spool ended. In the brief interval before the next one began, Woodthorpe coughed uneasily and muttered, "This was all long ago, Carey. The winds of change . . ."

"Are blowing up a real storm, Woodthorpe. You'll see why."

The tapes began again. A huge plant now stood at the

155

edge of the sea, distilling fresh water from the salt. A settlement had sprung up beside it, with fields and plantations of young trees.

"It has gone well," said the Rama voice. "It will go better with time, for their short generations move quickly."

The settlement became a city. The population grew, spread, built more cities, planted more crops. The land flourished.

"Many thousands live," the Rama said, "who would otherwise not have been born. We have repaid our murders."

The spool ended.

Woodthorpe said, "But we're not trying to atone for anything. We . . ."

"If my house burns down," said Carey, "I do not greatly care whether it was by a stroke of lightning, deliberate arson, or a child playing with matches. The end result is the same."

The third spool began.

A different voice spoke now. Carey wondered if the owner of the first had chosen death himself, or simply lacked the heart to go on with the record. The distilling plant was wearing out and metals for repair were poor and difficult to find. The solar batteries could not be replaced. The stream of water dwindled. Crops died. There was famine and panic, and then the pumps stopped altogether and the cities were stranded like the hulks of ships in dry harbors.

The Rama voice said, "These are the consequences of the one kind act we have ever done. Now these thousands that we called into life must die as their forebears did. The cruel laws of survival that we caused them to forget are all to be learned again. They had suffered once, and mastered it, and were content. Now there is nothing we can do to help. We can only stand and watch."

"Shut it off," said Woodthorpe.

"No," said Carey, "see it out."

They saw it out.

"Now," said Carey, "I will remind you that Kharif was the homeland from which most of the Drylands were settled." He was speaking to the Committee more than to Woodthorpe. "These so-called primitives have been through all this before, and they have long memories. Their tribal legends are explicit about what happened to them the last time they put their trust in the transitory works of men. Now can you understand why they're so determined to fight?"

Woodthorpe looked at the disturbed and frowning faces of the Committee. "But," he said, "it wouldn't be like that now. Our resources . . ."

"Are millions of miles away on other planets. How long can you guarantee to keep *your* pumps working? And the Ramas at least had left the natural water sources for the survivors to go back to. You want to destroy those so they would have nothing." Carey glanced at the men from the City-States. "The City-States would pay the price for that. They have the best of what there is, and with a large population about to die of famine and thirst . . ." He shrugged, and then went on, "There are other ways to help. Food and medicines. Education, to enable the young people to look for greener pastures in other places, if they wish to. In the meantime, there is an army on the move. You have the power to stop it. You've heard all there is to be said. Now the chiefs are waiting to hear what you will say."

The Chairman of the Committee conferred with the members. The conference was quite brief.

"Tell the chiefs," the Chairman said, "that it is not our intent to create wars. Tell them to go in peace. Tell them the Rehabilitation Project for Mars is canceled."

The great tide rolled slowly back into the Drylands and dispersed. Carey went through a perfunctory hearing on his activities, took his reprimand and dismissal with a light heart, shook hands with Howard Wales, and went back to Jekkara, to drink with Derech and walk beside the Low Canal that would be there now for whatever ages were left to it in the slow course of a planet's dying.

And this was good. But at the end of the canal was Barrakesh, and the southward-moving caravans, and the long road to Sinharat. Carey thought of the vaults beyond the fallen block of marble, and he knew that someday he would walk that road again.

CLASSICS OF GREAT SCIENCE-FICTION

from ACE BOOKS

Available from Ace Books, Inc. (Dept. MM), 1120 Avenue of the Americas, New York, N.Y. 10036. Send price indicated, plus 5¢ handling fee.

Andre Norton novels available

from Ace Books include:

GALACTIC DERELICT   (F-310)
THE BEAST MASTER   (F-315)
THE LAST PLANET   (M-151)
STORM OVER WARLOCK   (F-109)
SEA SIEGE   (F-147)
CATSEYE   (G-654)
THE DEFIANT AGENTS   (M-150)
STAR BORN   (M-148)
THE STARS ARE OURS!   (M-147)
WITCH WORLD   (G-655)
HUON OF THE HORN   (F-226)
STAR GATE   (M-157)
THE TIME TRADERS   (F-386)
LORD OF THUNDER   (F-243)
WEB OF THE WITCH WORLD   (F-263)
SHADOW HAWK   (G-538)
SARGASSO OF SPACE   (F-279)
JUDGMENT ON JANUS   (F-308)
PLAGUE SHIP   (F-291)
KEY OUT OF TIME   (F-287)
ORDEAL IN OTHERWHERE   (F-325)
NIGHT OF MASKS   (F-365)
QUEST CROSSTIME   (G-595)
STAR GUARD   (G-599)
YEAR OF THE UNICORN   (F-357)
THREE AGAINST THE WITCH WORLD (F-332)
THE SIOUX SPACEMAN   (F-408)
WARLOCK OF THE WITCH WORLD   (G-630)

(F-books are 40¢;   M-books are 45¢;   G-books are 50¢.)